Once Upon a Tee

Once Upon a Tee

A Golf Story

BY
William Willis

One Upon a Tee: A Golf Story
Copyright © 2016 William Willis

William Willis Books
11603 Wild Thicket
San Antonio, Texas 78254
210-218-6505
williamwillisauthor.com

ISBN-13
Print: 978-0-9894052-2-5
Ebook: 978-0-9894052-3-2

Cover Design: Aundrea Hernandez
Editors: Lillie Ammann, Jan McClintock

Also by William Willis

Base Jumping: The Vagabond Life of a Military Brat

✕

Dedication

For my dad, Sidney Augustine Willis, who taught me the fine art of caddying and the special relationship that exists between golfer and caddie

Acknowledgments

I'd like to thank my dad for the book title; he wrote a golf column entitled "Once Upon a Tee" for the Richards-Gebaur Air Force Base newspaper in the early 1960s.

Once again, I'd like to thank my fantastic editor, Lillie Ammann, and her magnificent assistant, Jan McClintock, for their invaluable assistance. As with my first book, they taught me so much about the art of writing. I would also like to thank Aundrea Hernandez for her help in designing the book cover. I look forward to working with them again.

The immutable truth, as old as the game itself, is that a golfer's skill must not flow from what he holds in his hands but from what he possesses in his head and heart.

~*Golf in America: The First One Hundred Years*, by George Peper and the Editors of *Golf Magazine*

And the load doesn't weigh me down at all. He ain't heavy, he's my brother.

~From the song "He Ain't Heavy, He's My Brother" by Bobby Scott and Bob Russell

Prologue

The depthless coal-black eyes peering through the rusty iron bars bored straight into the man's soul. *Cobra eyes*, he thought, as he lowered his emaciated and torn body to the earthen floor. *Menacing. Predatory. Pure evil.*

He'd spent two weeks in this cesspit of a cell, barely larger than his mother's pantry. *They can beat, torture, and humiliate me, but these Jap heathens will never control my mind.* The thought brought a quick laugh from his lips, but that came to an abrupt halt when pain seared his bruised ribs.

As if starvation and solitary confinement weren't enough, his captors delighted in beating him and the other prisoners with large sticks and rifle butts. Gingerly touching his rib cage, he figured that last session must have busted several ribs.

Losing control of your life is a frightening thing, the young man thought, as he tried, unsuccessfully, to settle into a more comfortable position.

I swear to God, if I manage to survive this ordeal, Heaven help the man who tries to keep me down again.

The only thing that kept him from going insane was re-living happy memories of golf outings with his father before this terrible war. As a kid, he had caddied for his dad. When he was old enough to play golf alongside his father, he felt he had passed a rite of manhood. Unfortunately, his real rite of manhood arrived a few years later in the form of a letter from the President of the United States with those chilling words, "Greetings..."

Before he left home to serve his country in "The Great Fight," as this terrible world war was sometimes called, his dad embraced him in a tearful farewell.

"Boudreaux, you once called me your hero because of the fighting I did in the Great War. Well, I have to say it looks like you're my hero now. Watch your back, come home safe, and make us proud. Before you know it, you'll be home, and we'll be chasing balls around the old course again."

Now, wasting away in a cell somewhere in the Pacific as a prisoner of war, Boudreaux wiped away the tears streaming down his face.

Some hero I turned out to be, Dad. I guess even heroes sometimes fail. I'm so sorry I let you down.

Chapter One

The small white dimpled sphere whizzed as it rose through the warm spring air like a soaring hawk riding a thermal updraft searching for prey. The tremendous collision of the brass-plated persimmon golf club and gutta-percha echoed through the tall live oaks, scattering a covey of quail hiding in the azalea bushes lining the tee box. The sunlit orb arced over the vast panorama of hills and dales, trees and grass, water and sand.

As the man picked up his tee, his steely gaze wandered over the early morning dew-covered grass of the perfectly manicured fairway.

How beautiful, he thought. *Almost as beautiful as the Tokyo Country Club course back home.*

That majestic gem of the Orient, with its unique, elevated double greens (one for summer, one for fall) would always be his favorite course. He would like to be able to return someday to that pillar of the Japanese golf world located in Sayama, northwest of Tokyo, but he realized that was unlikely to happen. Too many people might recognize him, even after the plastic surgery on his face.

He harbored bitter feelings over the reprehensible treatment of the course he had played regularly before he was yanked from his comfortable executive position with a large manufacturing firm and thrust into a uniform to serve the emperor. When the war began, the Japanese military commandeered the course for its own use. Even more distressing, after Japan's surrender, the United States occupational force appropriated it. When that force pulled out several years later, it was finally returned to its rightful owners, but he still felt that sacred ground was tainted.

The intoxicating smells of jasmine (though not as memorable as the smell of cherry blossoms in bloom in his beloved Japan) and fresh-mown grass wafted over him as he paused to enjoy the moment. He'd had enough of the horrors of war and seldom dwelt on the past, but it still occasionally haunted him in his dreams.

Truth be told, he was more the deliverer than the recipient of those wartime horrors. He still felt his actions were justified. After all, wasn't he just doing his job? He noticed his caddie staring at him.

Enough of this negativity, he thought as he blinked.

The man was resplendent in his beautifully tailored, tan cashmere sweater, hounds-tooth plus fours, and argyle socks. He bore a smug smile as his ball rolled to a stop, as always, in the middle of the fairway. Snapping his fingers impatiently, he motioned for his caddie to light his expensive cigar and ordered the young man to hand him his 7 iron. His smooth, effortless shot dropped the ball to within a few feet of the pin, leaving him a short putt for a birdie.

Except for his caddie, he was alone, but he was not a lonely man. He preferred to practice for big tournaments without anyone else around. Already a world-class amateur, he avoided playing with those he deemed inferior, saving his few group outings for those in his elevated social circle.

His goal this year was to qualify for the United States Open Golf Championship as an amateur, a formidable feat, then turn his sights to a professional career. After that, he would show the world he was the best to ever play the game. The passion to be the first Asian player to dominate the golf world burned within him.

Nobody knew much about this strange, diminutive, yet powerful man. He claimed he was from somewhere in California, but revealed little of his past. He had few friends but proudly showcased a beautiful Asian wife, who was equally as mysterious. He was enormously wealthy, and when big money talks, people ask few questions. He seemed to buy relationships rather than to cultivate them, especially in the case of his trophy wife.

His dark complexion and lack of an accent made even his nationality a question mark. He spoke with perfect diction and displayed a wide range of knowledge, demonstrating an excellent education. His manners were impeccable, except when dealing with servants and caddies. He was, in short, an enigma.

As he walked to the next tee, he caught a flash of light reflected from the tree line about a hundred yards down the left side of the fairway. Momentarily puzzled, he shrugged and teed his golf ball. As he began his backswing, he saw it again.

That's odd, he thought.

His curiosity piqued, after teeing off he wandered over to the spot where the flash of light came from. He found nothing except trampled grass and a small plume of smoke coming from a stubbed-out cigarette.

Someone was here watching me. Who could it have been? Hmm... No. No way could anybody find me after all this time.

A few yards away behind a hedge, Boudreaux gasped.

"It's him, Johnny. I'm sure of it," he whispered. "After all these years, he turns up in our own backyard."

"Are you sure, Boudreaux?" Johnny cocked his head. "It sure doesn't look like the same slimy maggot we all loved so well."

"The eyes, Johnny. Look at the eyes. He has those same cobra eyes. I'd recognize them anywhere. I see them every night." Boudreaux took a deep breath. "The face is different, somehow. Cosmetic surgery, maybe. But there's no disguising the evil in those eyes. It's him. I'm sure of it."

Chapter Two

On Good Friday, April 3, 1942, Boudreaux James realized his life was probably coming to an end.

"Come on, Sergeant, if we don't move soon, we're gonna be burned alive!" he shouted to his squad leader from his foxhole.

His complaint fell on deaf ears, for Sergeant Bates was already a blur of dust, knees, and elbows darting through artillery fire for the cover of the jungle. Or at least, what was left of the jungle from the incendiary bombs the Japanese planes were dropping.

It took Boudreaux less than two seconds to follow suit, trying to keep up with his fearless leader. After they reunited and squatted in what little foliage wasn't on fire, they tried to make sense out of this nightmare.

Boudreaux turned to look at Bates.

"What do we do now?"

"We try to regroup with whoever we can find alive and wait for instructions from the general," Sergeant Bates replied. "I don't know if you're a praying man, Boudreaux, but, if not, now would be a good time to change that."

On December 22, 1941, two weeks after the Japanese attack on Pearl Harbor, pandemonium had reigned along the Leyte Gulf in the Philippines. General Masaharu Homma had led a massive Japanese invasion of the country. Since then, Boudreaux's division had been making a valiant but futile attempt to defend a beach position seventy-five miles north of the Bataan Peninsula on the South China Sea.

For the next three and a half months, they fought bravely but accomplished little more than trading fire and lives like some senseless chess match. With Japanese reinforcements brought in almost daily, the Americans were severely outnumbered. Eventually, they were forced southward until they were trapped in the middle of the peninsula. There, on April 3, 1942, Boudreaux was given a formal introduction to war. Savage artillery fire, bombs, and incendiary fire had him convinced he would never see his family again.

General Edward P. King, commander of the forces at Bataan, soon realized resistance would lead only to the slaughter of his men. On April 8, 1942, he made the anguished decision to surrender. Boudreaux and his comrades looked to their uncertain fate with terror, when General King led his men, under a flag of truce, down the jungle trail to the town of Cabcaben.

Boudreaux was a good ole boy from the south and an avid student of American Civil War history. He couldn't escape the irony that General Robert E. Lee had surrendered to General Ulysses S. Grant at Appomattox on this date in 1865.

The next day, while the defeated soldiers awaited the unknown, Japanese soldiers appeared at 6:30 a.m.

"Looks like we're done for," Boudreaux said to Sergeant Bates, who warily surveyed the enemy.

Their enemies showed contempt for the American soldiers because the Japanese believed that any soldier who would choose to surrender rather than take his own life was a disgrace and a coward. The Japanese unceremoniously stripped the Americans of their valuables while a Japanese corporal ordered his men to kick and slap their captives.

Bayonet-wielding soldiers forced the fifty or so men in Boudreaux's group to march northward. Shortly thereafter, they were joined by several hundred more American soldiers, exhausted and dispirited. Occasionally, convoys of southbound trucks carrying Japanese soldiers passed them. Some of the crueler Japanese soldiers forced the prisoners to pick up the pace by striking them with sticks and rifle butts, adding to their fear and humiliation.

Over the next few days, the ranks of American and Filipino prisoners swelled to many thousands. In groups of one hundred, they were lined up in four columns, guarded by eight to ten Japanese guards.

As Boudreaux stumbled along, the appearance of his captors surprised him. These diminutive men were barely five feet tall and wore khaki uniforms with leggings. Their cloth caps had flaps covering their necks.

"I can't believe we've been taken by a bunch of midgets," Boudreaux mumbled to no one in particular.

The Japanese soldiers kept pressing their captives forward, providing neither food nor water. Stragglers and those who begged for water were clubbed. Several prisoners who bolted from their ranks to drink water from a roadside ditch were shot and killed.

By nightfall, after marching fifteen miles, they arrived at the town of Balanga. They were corralled in a small barbed-wire pen, many suffering from malaria and diarrhea as well as thirst and hunger. The weary captives were allowed to stand in line for a brief drink of water from a single faucet.

Despite their attempt to get some rest, at midnight they were ordered to resume marching. Shortly afterward, the wind picked up and rain started to fall. Boudreaux shivered uncontrollably.

He noticed that, due to the rapid pace set by the guards, some of the prisoners struggled to keep from losing their shoes in the mud. He tried to help them, but many ended up barefoot.

At dawn, they arrived at the town of Orani, having covered ten more grueling miles. A few hours later, Boudreaux and the others were herded into another dirty, crowded barbed-wire pen. They were exposed to the baking sun for the remainder of the day. They were given a handful of rice, the first food Boudreaux had eaten in a day and a half.

Boudreaux struggled to get comfortable enough to get some sleep inside the cramped quarters reeking of human waste. Early the next morning, they were roused and forced to line up again. Their ranks had dwindled—several of the weaker prisoners had died during the night.

Their next march ended at Lubao, a small town twenty miles north. For the third night in a row, Boudreaux and the others were put inside a barbed-wire enclosure. They drank water from a single faucet and ate the small portions of rice doled out by their captors. By the next morning, many more had perished.

Will this insanity ever end? Boudreaux thought. *I don't think I can take much more of this.*

The next day's march ended around noon in the larger town of San Fernando, nearly twenty miles further north. The number of survivors had dwindled even further as weakened men fell behind or were shot or beaten to death by unsympathetic guards. There was no layover here.

The prisoners were paraded through town under the forlorn gazes of Filipino citizens. Boudreaux saw a few cautiously showing their support by flashing the two-fingered "V" sign for victory or nodding their heads slightly. They understood the Americans were doing their best to liberate their country from their Japanese oppressors. Now they were forced to stand by helplessly and watch their liberators being beaten and murdered.

Tears came to Boudreaux's eyes when he passed a small group of boys smiling and humming "God Bless America." The swell of pride Boudreaux felt was interrupted by a shove from a guard, who ordered the prisoners to board small railroad freight cars.

"Riding in this train will be an improvement over walking," Boudreaux said to an older man standing next to him.

"Don't be so sure, young fella," the man said. "Take a look at how small those boxcars are and how many of us there are."

The man is right, Boudreaux thought.

The men were crammed so tightly into the steel-sided boxcars that breathing was next to impossible. With no room to sit down, no water, and the sun's rays heating up his confined space, Boudreaux was near collapse.

During the sweltering twenty-eight-mile trip north, many more men died, some from dehydration and others from suffocation. When the train arrived at the town of Capas, the survivors were taken off and forced to march eight miles westward to a former Philippine Army training camp called Camp O'Donnell. Enclosed by strands of barbed wire, it had been converted into a Japanese prisoner of war camp.

The date was April 12, 1942, the fourth and final day of the arduous trek across the Bataan Peninsula. Future historians would memorialize this trek as the Bataan Death March. As many as 1,500 American and approximately 10,000 Filipino soldiers died on that journey.

Fear and trepidation filled Boudreaux's heart when the camp's huge gate slammed shut. He thought back to the religious advice Sergeant Bates had given him four days ago: *Okay, Lord. My life is in your hands. What do you have up your sleeve now?*

Chapter Three

Camp O'Donnell, surrounded by great expanses of grassy fields, was a square compound protected at each corner with bamboo guard towers. The long and narrow barracks housing the prisoners were made of bamboo with thatched roofs.

This compound became Boudreaux's home for the next two months. It was also where he met the man who would not only save his life on several occasions but would become the greatest friend he ever had. In this pestilent prison, where nearly 2,000 of the 9,000 American prisoners would eventually die from starvation, malaria, and dysentery, these two men would be among the few to survive. Their survival was due in large part to an unbreakable bond they forged during this desperate time.

When he first saw the other man, Boudreaux wasn't impressed. Standing six feet four inches tall and weighing 230 pounds, Boudreaux towered over the slightly built man almost half a foot shorter than himself. That impression changed the first time their eyes met. This small man with the penetrating blue eyes introduced himself as Sergeant Johnny Frye. Johnny's self-confidence and scrappy attitude inspired Boudreaux.

Most of the prisoners appeared frightened and beaten. Not Sergeant Frye. Instead, his clenched jaws and icy demeanor gave him the look of someone who was really ticked off. His quick, darting eyes seemed to take in everything around him, as if he were planning his next move. Boudreaux had a feeling that this man would not let these Japanese guards break him. He was someone to be reckoned with. He was also a man Boudreaux wanted on his side. If he were going to survive this ordeal, it would be wise to latch onto someone stronger than himself.

Johnny had an air of authority that had a calming effect on those around him. This quality garnered the respect of his fellow prisoners, especially the senior officers. This unusual man was only twenty-seven years old.

"I'm Boudreaux James, Sergeant Frye," Boudreaux said, wanting to get on his good side as soon as possible.

"Call me Johnny, please. Under the circumstances, I'd say we're all equals around here," Johnny said with a quick laugh.

How can anyone laugh in a place like this? Boudreaux thought.

In groups of men, it's not unusual for someone with determination and the sheer will to live to find ways to survive. Such was the case with Johnny. He quickly became the one who figured out a way to use work details outside the camp to make contact with Filipino locals, acquiring extra food and scarce medicines. No one knew his secret. Most likely, his success was a combination of wit, self-assurance, and pure nerve that enabled him to accomplish things that others could not.

Boudreaux, at age eighteen, was a naive, unworldly kid who, despite his size, had no clue how to survive in this strange environment. The only son of a middle-class hardware store owner, he could not understand how the Japanese soldiers could harbor such hatred for Americans and treat them with so much hostility. He was terrified and confused and feared he wouldn't fare well here. The cruel guards picked up on the weaknesses of young, sensitive prisoners like Boudreaux and seemed to delight in doling out unmerciful punishment for every minor infraction of camp rules.

"The number one rule around here is to survive at all costs," Johnny said. "The number two rule is to keep your big mouth shut around the captain and the guards. I've heard the guards have already beaten several prisoners to death."

For the next few weeks, Johnny looked after Boudreaux and taught him the basics of survival. While he appreciated Johnny's help, Boudreaux couldn't understand why the man took such an interest in the welfare of a hotheaded kid.

Johnny seemed to have a knack for doing the impossible. While other prisoners were fighting boredom, starvation, and general lack of spirit, Johnny hustled. It was like he was playing a game instead of fighting for his life. He scoured the compound, catching rats, insects, snakes, stray cats and dogs—anything that could be used for food. Perhaps this was a result of his spartan upbringing.

Reluctant at first, Boudreaux soon found that he could eat anything if he was hungry enough. Johnny also taught Boudreaux the importance of staying in the center of groups of prisoners to avoid being picked on by the guards. Boudreaux learned a lot from his new friend and protector.

He was, however, a little suspicious of Johnny's motives. One evening, while the two of them were sharing a banana Johnny had smuggled into camp following a work detail, Boudreaux's curiosity got the better of him.

"Why are you helping me, Johnny?" Boudreaux asked. "What's in it for you? You're not one of them guys who, uh…you know what I mean?"

"No," Johnny replied, laughing at Boudreaux's bluntness. "You ain't exactly my type."

Johnny suddenly seemed to lose his concentration as he stared vacantly at the ground. Boudreaux detected a strange sadness enveloping his friend.

"What is it, Johnny?" Boudreaux asked cautiously.

"It's hard for me to even talk about this," Johnny said.

Boudreaux was alarmed to see tears forming in the corners of Johnny's eyes.

"I have a little brother. He's about your age. When war broke out, he decided he wasn't about to be upstaged by his big brother. Though I tried to talk him into joining the Navy or the Coast Guard, the hardheaded fool joined the Army. This past March, I got a letter from my folks saying he was reported missing in action somewhere in Malaysia. Nobody's heard a word from him since. I don't know if he's dead or held captive in another camp like this one. He's the only brother I've got, Boudreaux, and you sort of remind me of him. I'm praying he's alive somewhere. Even if he's in a prisoner of war camp, he has a chance to get back home."

"If he's anything like you, Johnny, I'm sure he's alive."

"Boudreaux, he's just a kid. All the Army teaches you about what to do if you're captured is give your name, rank, and serial number. They don't teach you squat about how to survive. I taught my brother how to be a woodsman, but, unfortunately, this is a whole different ballgame." He shook his head.

"I made a pact with the Lord when I met you, Boudreaux," Johnny continued. "I told Him that if my little brother is in a camp like this one, and if He will send him a guardian angel to watch over him, I'll do the same for you. I'm going to be your guardian angel, Boudreaux, and you're going to be my salvation as well as my little brother's. You have to make it for all our sakes."

Boudreaux looked away, uncomfortable seeing his friend like this. Johnny suddenly broke down and started crying. Hesitantly, Boudreaux knelt by Johnny's side and placed a soothing hand on his heaving shoulder.

"Don't worry, Johnny," Boudreaux said. "We'll get through this. I'm sure your brother is alive and well, just waiting for the chance to get back home to do a little more hunting and fishing with his big brother."

During their stay at Camp O'Donnell, the bond between Boudreaux and Johnny grew stronger. It must have looked peculiar to the other prisoners—a large, stocky young man being watched over and protected by a skinny, wiry man half his size.

On June 2, 1942, the camp commander announced that the approximately 7,000 prisoners were being transferred to another camp. Leaving the mass graves of 2,000 Americans behind, they boarded trucks for the ride back to the rail siding at Capas. They were squeezed into the same cramped box cars that had brought them there two months earlier. They traveled north ten miles to the small town of Cabanatuan, and, fortunately, the train's doors were left open this time. After exiting the train, they were marched five miles to Camp Cabanatuan. If Boudreaux thought conditions couldn't be any worse, he was in for a rude awakening. His nightmare was just beginning.

✕ Chapter Four

Boudreaux's morale initially improved when it appeared that conditions at Camp Cabanatuan were better than those at Camp O'Donnell. Several faucets provided adequate drinking water and open wells provided enough water for laundry and bathing.

The new arrivals were greeted by other prisoners captured earlier on the island of Corregidor off the southern coast of the Bataan Peninsula. These men showed the same shocking symptoms that Boudreaux saw in the men he arrived with—dramatic weight loss, sunken eyes, and forlorn, distant expressions.

To Boudreaux's dismay, conditions went from bad to worse during the twenty-seven months he was incarcerated there. The rampant cruelty and beatings continued. Lack of nutrition and medicine resulted in a casualty rate of twenty-five to thirty men per day. Boudreaux suffered from malaria, dysentery, and scurvy. He would have died if not for Johnny's aid.

The guards selected men for various work details, some of which were away from the camp. Johnny was one of the fortunate ones to get to work as a stevedore loading ships at the Manila docks. On those excursions, Johnny, again using his wits and cunning, managed to smuggle in small amounts of fruit, vegetables, and meat. He even found a source of quinine, which helped Boudreaux combat the effects of malaria.

Johnny knew he would be shot if caught but was willing to take the chance if it meant easing the misery of his friend. These items he managed to procure from sympathetic Filipino farmers. Despite the immense risk to themselves, they had not forgotten the Americans who valiantly attempted to liberate their country.

Boudreaux was overcome with emotion at Johnny's risk-taking on his behalf. He made a promise to himself that, should they both survive, he would repay Johnny many times over for these acts of kindness. His health gradually improved as a result of Johnny's care.

Johnny generously shared some of the smuggled food with the weaker prisoners. Word spread through the camp of Johnny's selflessness. Respect for Johnny grew, and he acquired a reputation as something of a savior. In keeping with his laid-back, unassuming demeanor, Johnny just shrugged it off.

"As soon as this war is over, you fellows will forget all about me," he said. "Anyway, where I come from, neighbors look out for one another."

Boudreaux's admiration and gratitude for the things Johnny did further cemented their friendship, making them as close as brothers. Boudreaux and Johnny worked day after day in the rice fields and wondered when all this madness would end. Eventually, even the ever-optimistic Johnny started to show signs of giving up.

"Why don't they just shoot us and get it over with?" he asked Boudreaux one morning, despair creeping into his voice.

That night, rumors circulated that American planes had bombed several Japanese installations. The biggest rumor circulating in mid-October 1944 was that General Douglas MacArthur had returned to the Philippines, as he had promised, to exact revenge on the Japanese and to rescue all prisoners of war.

In late October, despite Boudreaux's optimism that the United States finally had the Japanese on the run, the prisoners' situation turned much worse. They were told to prepare to move. Another rumor circulated that their destination was Japan.

"That doesn't make any sense," Johnny said. "If they're losing the war, why not let us go?"

"Johnny, I heard that the Japanese never release prisoners of war." Boudreaux said quietly. "They execute them. We're going to die."

Chapter Five

The ruthless guards loaded the prisoners onto trucks for the seven-hour ride to Bilibid Prison in Manila. During the trip, Boudreaux gazed at the skyline of Manila in the distance. Its transformation shocked him. Where once a beautiful, thriving city pulsed, lay a mass of destruction. Bomb-shattered buildings dotted the landscape. Very little had survived the Japanese invaders.

The prisoners remained in Bilibid Prison under guard for two months. In December 1944, Boudreaux, Johnny, and the approximately 1,600 remaining prisoners were loaded onto the Japanese freighter *Brazil Maru*. They were confined in the crowded holds below decks, while the upper decks were filled with Japanese families.

"They know they're losing the war," Johnny said. "That's why they're high-tailing it for home. I wouldn't be surprised if they were planning to use us as hostages to get better terms when they surrender."

"Let's just hope we live that long," Boudreaux said.

The dark, cramped holds held barely enough air to breathe and space to sit down. Boudreaux and Johnny stayed together to prevent being separated in the foul-smelling mass of bodies. They had survived this long by supporting each other physically and emotionally. They weren't about to lose track of each other now. If they died, they would do it together.

With the shortage of fresh air, chaos ensued. Men panicked, cursed, and shoved each other. Oftentimes in a catastrophic situation, an unlikely hero will emerge and take charge. It could be anyone: a gallant officer, a lowly private, a clerk typist. One never knows what brings out the best in a man. Boudreaux wasn't all that surprised when Johnny proved to be that man. With the authority of a commanding general, he climbed halfway up the ladder to the lower hold and demanded everyone's attention. The commotion stopped long enough for Johnny to explain the importance of staying calm.

"Men, I'm asking you to please stop yelling and shoving. There's barely enough air as it is. The more you yell and move around, the more oxygen you use up. Stay quiet and still. That increases everyone's chance of survival. The war's almost over. If we pull together and stay calm, we may get out of this yet."

With his impassioned pleas, the men settled down. Later, small buckets of rice and fish soup were lowered into the hold. It wasn't much, but it was enough to fend off starvation. Still, many prisoners died the first night from suffocation and unbearable heat.

In late January 1945, after six weeks of despondency and misery, the ship docked on the northern coast of Kyushu, Japan in the small seaport of Moji. The captives were taken by truck to nearby Camp Fukuoka #17, one of many prisoner of war camps in Japan. Of the approximately 9,000 Americans brought to Camp O'Donnell in 1942, only a little over 1,100 survived to make it to Japan.

The prisoners were shorn of beard and hair and deloused. Boudreaux and Johnny noticed that the prisoners already imprisoned there looked like little more than skeletons—bony arms and legs, rib cages protruding grotesquely, eyes fixed, unseeing, on the ground.

The new arrivals were assigned to cells inside unheated, wooden barracks. Beds were wooden platforms covered with straw and paper sheets. Inadequate meals were served twice daily and usually consisted of seaweed or radish soup and rice. Occasionally, barley was provided. Diarrhea and mistreatment from cruel and stupid guards were constant problems.

In February 1945, Tokyo was bombed by American B-29s. Shortly after that, other Japanese cities were bombed as well. Though the situation looked bad for Japan—rumors of an invasion by the Americans circulated—the emperor would not surrender. War still raged, and treatment of the prisoners worsened.

Chapter Six

Captain Akio Funaki, the camp commander at Fukuoka #17, showed total disregard for the Geneva Convention of 1929, which prohibited inhumane treatment of prisoners of war. Like all patriotic Japanese soldiers, Captain Funaki believed in death before dishonor. Surrendering was an act of cowardice and the most dishonorable act a soldier could commit. For that reason, he viewed all prisoners as cowards who did not deserve the fair treatment decreed by the Geneva Convention.

Captain Funaki held great contempt for all the prisoners, but his acute hatred for the Americans may have been fueled by the fact that most of them were at least a head taller than the captain and the guards. Those with deep feelings of inferiority about size sometimes exhibit a Napoleon complex, feeling a strong need to degrade others who remind them of their shortcomings. Since the Americans appeared to be the largest men in camp, they were obvious targets of his rage.

During an early morning inspection, Captain Funaki paused in front of a trembling Boudreaux. Noting his towering height, Funaki smiled contemptuously and asked him his name.

"Boudreaux James, sir," Boudreaux answered.

"Budo, what kind of crazy name is that?" Funaki asked, unable to pronounce Boudreaux's name correctly.

Boudreaux was astonished that the captain spoke passable English.

Funaki continued, "My name is Akio. It means glorious warrior in Japanese. What does Budo mean, cowardly dog?"

Boudreaux remained silent.

"You are surprised I speak English?" Captain Funaki said to a shocked Boudreaux. "My father forced me to go to university in your wretched country for two long years before the war. Just long enough to find out just how inferior your culture is."

Boudreaux resisted the urge to pound the smirk off the captain's face with his huge fist, knowing that would be suicide.

Instead, unable to contain his anger, he blurted, "You'll find out how inferior it is when we wipe Japan off the face of the earth."

Before Boudreaux could react, Captain Funaki swung a large wooden stick he drew from behind his back and connected with the side of Boudreaux's head. The blow sent Boudreaux sprawling, face first, into the dirt. After delivering several more vicious blows to Boudreaux's body, Captain Funaki ordered two guards to carry his limp body to a small isolation cell.

After struggling to a sitting position, Boudreaux saw the contemptuous, evil eyes of the captain peering through the bars. After a few seconds, the captain spun on his heels and walked away. Boudreaux was kept there for two weeks. Apparently, this was intended to demonstrate to all prisoners that anything other than total obedience would not be tolerated.

After his two weeks of solitary incarceration, Boudreaux was carried out by guards, half dead, and dumped on the ground. Johnny picked up a filthy and emaciated Boudreaux and carried him to his barracks. He carefully placed him on one of the bamboo-covered platforms that served as a bed and cleaned the wound to his head with a damp cloth.

"Take it easy, Boudreaux. The war can't last much longer. When Japan surrenders, he'll be sure to hang for all the war crimes he committed." Johnny smiled. "By the way," he asked. "Where did you get a crazy name like Budo—I mean Boudreaux?"

"It's an old Cajun name. My dad's family is from the bayous of Louisiana. He couldn't stand living in the swamps any longer, so after the Great War, he moved to San Antonio, Texas, and settled there. That's where I was born and raised. What about you? I don't recall you talking much about where you come from."

"I come from a small farm in the middle of the Ozark Mountains of Missouri," Johnny said. "For a kid, it was paradise—camping, hunting, and fishing with my old man and my little brother, living off the land and learning to be self-sufficient. But, as I got older, the isolation sort of got to me. When I turned eighteen, I joined the Army to see the world. That was in 1933. For the last twelve years, I've been living the Army life and seeing places my folks never even heard of. Of course, these five-star establishments we've been staying in the last three years weren't exactly in my itinerary."

Boudreaux laughed, suddenly realizing he couldn't remember the last time he'd had a reason to laugh at anything.

They both tried to remain inconspicuous by staying in the middle of the crowd of prisoners whenever possible.

After Boudreaux's last exchange with Funaki, he knew he probably wouldn't survive another encounter with him.

Unfortunately, Johnny was unable to escape Funaki's wrath. One afternoon, Funaki attempted to single out Boudreaux again for further *obedience training*. Johnny intervened on his friend's behalf, pleading with the captain to spare his friend. In response, Funaki turned on Johnny, delivering a blow that knocked him unconscious. In a rage, he brought the bloody stick down on Johnny's head over and over. One of the guards saved Johnny's life by pleading with Funaki to stop.

After Funaki returned to his office, Boudreaux carried Johnny's limp body back to his bed, where he did his best to clean his wounds.

"Aw, Johnny," Boudreaux cried, cradling his friend's head in his lap. "I'm sorry. I'm so sorry. This is all my fault."

Johnny's cuts and bruises healed, but he just wasn't the same old Johnny. For several months, Boudreaux kept a close eye on his friend. Johnny's condition improved, but Boudreaux could tell that something was just not quite right with Johnny mentally and physically. He could talk and take care of himself, but he was a little slower in getting around and grasping the meaning of things.

He's probably suffered some kind of brain damage, Boudreaux thought. *Hopefully, it's temporary. If not, I'll take care of him myself. He saved my life again. I owe him for that.*

On the first and second days of August 1945, American B-29 bombers dropped millions of leaflets over Japanese cities warning that if the emperor did not surrender, heavy bombing would commence. By August 6, no surrender was forthcoming, so a B-29 dropped an atomic bomb on the city of Hiroshima. A large portion of the city was leveled and over 100,000 people died.

By August 9, the emperor still had refused to surrender, and another atomic bomb was dropped. This one destroyed most of Nagasaki, with another great loss of life. This second explosion was only thirty-five miles from Camp Fukuoka #17.

Boudreaux had heard rumors of a great new bomb nearly destroying Hiroshima, but he was skeptical. His doubts vanished when he saw on the distant horizon a roiling, blue-gray mushroom-shaped cloud forming far to the southwest. When one of the guards told Boudreaux that that explosion was thirty-five miles away, he was stunned. He became a believer in man's capability to wipe out mankind.

"Johnny, what's happening to our world?" he asked his friend while lying on his bed. "First this crazy war, and now we've developed bombs that can blow up entire cities. I don't like it. I know it will end this war, but what about the next one we get into? I'm afraid for all of us, Johnny. I think maybe you're better off the way you are now."

Emperor Hirohito, to keep Japan from being annihilated, wisely decided to surrender. On August 20, 1945, after eleven days of utter confusion, Captain Akio Funaki handed over his sword to the senior ranking American prisoner of war. It was finally over. Amid cheers and whistles from the liberated prisoners, Boudreaux felt tremendous pride and relief. They were going home at last. He looked around and noticed all the guards milling around, looking bewildered and confused. Funaki had disappeared, but something on the ground near where he had surrendered his sword caught

Boudreaux's eye. It was the dreaded stick that Funaki had used to enforce discipline in the camp.

Boudreaux picked it up and turned it over and over in his hands. His thoughts swirled. He thought of the other men Funaki had beaten with it. He thought of the vicious beating he had endured. More importantly, he thought of the life-changing thrashing his friend, Johnny, had suffered while trying to protect him. He sat in the dirt and cried.

When he returned to his barracks, he carried the stick with him. For the duration of his stay there, he never let it out of his sight. This would be no mere war souvenir.

Funaki, no matter how long it takes, I'm going to find you. If the authorities don't hang you for your war crimes first, I'm going to beat you to death with your own stick.

On September 2, 1945, Japan formally surrendered. At the war crimes courts, many high-ranking Japanese officials and officers were found guilty of war crimes and sentenced to prison or hanged. Funaki was a suspected war criminal, but until he was found, he would go unpunished.

Several weeks later, Boudreaux and Johnny, with all the other liberated prisoners of war, were flown home on American planes. Among Boudreaux's few belongings was a crimson-colored stick that he cradled in his lap. He kept one eye on it and the other eye on his best friend dozing in the seat next to him.

"Rest up, my weary friend," Boudreaux said to Johnny. "I promised you I'd take care of you as long as I'm alive. But I've got big plans for the future, and I'm going to need your help. I believe God saved us for a reason, and I'm not going to let Him down. I also made a promise to myself, to you, and to the other men who suffered at the hands of Funaki. I will find him and he will pay for what he did."

Tears formed in Boudreaux's eyes as he scraped a thumbnail across the coarse blood-stained wood of Funaki's stick and put his arm around Johnny's shoulder.

Chapter Seven

"It hasn't changed much, Johnny," Boudreaux said, as he eased the car he'd borrowed from his Aunt Tilda up the winding, tree-lined drive. "The last time I saw this place I was twelve years old."

It was the spring of 1946. The beautiful Texas bluebonnets and Indian paintbrush were in full bloom, bathing the hillsides in a burst of blue, orange, and scarlet. Towering live oaks, some hundreds of years old, shared space with the small Texas mountain laurels with their violet-blue, grape-soda-scented flowers.

Boudreaux had forgotten how beautiful the Texas Hill Country was. His father had first brought him to the Whispering Hollows Country Club, renowned for its championship golf course, when he was a wide-eyed, eight-year-old kid. Too young to play, he had begged his dad to take him along just so he could hang out with his old man for the day.

Located near the small town of Kerrville, fifty miles northwest of San Antonio, it was the ideal getaway for visitors eager to escape the stress and uncertainty of post-World War II America. This was precisely the reason for Boudreaux's and Johnny's visit. Disillusioned with the world at large and scarred from the memories of their oppressive captivity during the war, he and Johnny wanted nothing more than to retreat from the outside world and be left alone.

Boudreaux figured it would take time for them to recuperate and get their lives back to normal. Mentally, Johnny seemed to be doing okay. It had taken him several months to get over the trauma of Funaki's beating and regain his confidence and irreverent, laid-back demeanor. Unfortunately, the beating had caused nerve damage in his left arm and leg. This resulted in a noticeable limp and an inability to lift heavy objects with his left hand.

The Army doctors said with time and exercise, Johnny might regain most of his mobility. Boudreaux, nine years younger than Johnny, had bounced back quickly from his beatings and mistreatment. His only reminder of the beatings was an improperly healed bone in his left wrist. Unable to bend it fully, he worried about how it would affect his golf swing. Boudreaux looked on Johnny as a brother and was committed to sticking by his side as long as Johnny needed him.

Upon his liberation from Camp Fukuoka #17, Boudreaux had been informed by his debriefing officer that his father had died from cancer in the summer of 1944. His father's medical expenses had depleted the family's meager savings and forced the sale of the hardware store at a loss. When the family was unable to make mortgage payments, the bank foreclosed on their home. Boudreaux's mom had to move in with her younger sister, Tilda, and her family. Two months after his father's death, his mother died suddenly. They didn't know the cause, but some relatives believed she died from a broken heart after first thinking she'd lost her son and then the shock of losing her husband.

Johnny called his parents and told them he was alive and well. He asked if they had received any word of his little brother. He was dismayed to learn that his brother was still missing in action. Because of his poor physical condition, he was afraid to return home. He wasn't sure how his parents would react to seeing him like this. Because of his stubborn pride, he decided to wait for his condition to improve before he visited them.

Upon his return to San Antonio, Boudreaux had asked his Aunt Tilda if he and Johnny could stay with her family until he figured out what he and Johnny were going to do. They helped by doing odd jobs around the house (jobs were scarce in San Antonio), but Boudreaux and Johnny felt like they were imposing.

In March, Boudreaux decided to drive out to the Whispering Hollows Country Club to look for work. He was still thinking about pursuing a career in golf, and what better place to start than at a golf course.

Especially one surrounded by miles of lush meadows, rolling hills, and forests of oak, mesquite, and cedar trees.

The day before, Boudreaux had called Augie Henderson, the club's head greenskeeper, about jobs for both Johnny and him. Augie had been a friend of Boudreaux's dad, who loved to play there. Boudreaux didn't know if Augie would remember the skinny little kid who tagged along with his dad, but it was worth a shot. Augie had understood that jobs were difficult to come by for returning vets and agreed to meet with Boudreaux and Johnny. He said he would see what he could do to help them.

An attendant working in the pro shop directed them to Augie's office in the back of the building. After a heads-up from the attendant, Augie was waiting for them at the door to his office and greeted them with a warm handshake.

"Boudreaux, good to see you again," Augie said with a hint of a British accent. "You look just like your old man." He looked a little shocked when he saw the frail-looking man shuffling along beside Boudreaux.

"Thanks for seeing us, Mr. Henderson."

"Please, call me Augie. Sorry to hear about your parents. They were good people."

"Thanks. This is my friend, Johnny. We both could sure use a job, Augie. We'll take anything you've got. We need to get out of my aunt's house. She's been great to us, but she's got a family of her own to take care of, and I feel we're just a burden."

"Pleasure meeting you, Johnny," Augie said, extending his hand. "Listen, I can get both of you work doing course maintenance as well as some odd jobs around the clubhouse. It won't pay much, but it will be steady."

"Thanks, Augie. We appreciate it," Boudreaux said with a relieved look on his face.

"I am concerned about one thing, though." Augie glanced in Johnny's direction. "Johnny, no offense intended, but I noticed you were limping as you came in. This job involves quite a bit of strenuous activity and some heavy lifting. Do you think you can handle it?"

"Yes sir, I can handle whatever you need me to do," Johnny replied. "I'm getting better every day."

"If you don't mind my asking, how did you get injured?"

Johnny and Boudreaux exchanged glances followed by an uncomfortable silence. It became obvious to Augie he was treading on a sensitive subject.

"Johnny's memory is still a little hazy over the details," Boudreaux said. "If you've got a little time, I can explain what happened."

Over the next hour, Boudreaux gave Augie the horrifying details of the events they both endured at the hands of the Japanese from the day they met until the day they were liberated from their last POW camp. Boudreaux stressed the role Johnny played in Boudreaux's survival as well as that of the many other soldiers whose lives he saved.

Augie sat in stunned silence while he took in the incredible story of their capture, incarceration, and torture. Without saying a word, he rose from his chair and slowly walked to the tall, dust-covered bookshelf in the corner. He reached up and brought down a worn, leather-covered photo album, gingerly laying it down on his desk. When Augie opened it, the first thing that caught Boudreaux's eye was a faded, black-and-white photograph of a group of men in dated, British Army uniforms.

"That handsome young fella on the left is yours truly," Augie said with a slight catch in his voice. "I volunteered for service in the King's Army to fight in the Great War. It was supposed to be the war that ended all wars. I guess you saw how that turned out."

"Dad never mentioned you served in World War I, too," Boudreaux said.

"I signed up in 1915. Like your dad, I wasn't about to stand by and watch Kaiser Wilhelm trample over Europe with his German hordes. We didn't talk much about our time over there, but we understood each other. We always felt a shared brotherhood.

"We were among the lucky ones to come home after it ended. Many of our friends didn't make it, and a lot of those who did make it home..." Augie's voice cracked as he glanced in Johnny's direction. "A lot of them left a little of themselves on the battlefield."

Augie walked out from behind his desk and gave Johnny, and then Boudreaux, long bear hugs. "You two can start Monday morning at seven o'clock, but tonight we drink."

Augie opened the bottom right drawer of his desk and brought out three glasses and a bottle of Canadian whiskey. He filled each glass half full and the three of them raised their drinks in a toast. "To the men who gave their all."

A few minutes later, Augie pulled Boudreaux aside. "I want you to keep a close eye on Johnny. I'll do everything I can to help him, but the owner may interfere if he thinks Johnny isn't pulling his weight. He might need a little help from time to time. Can you handle that?"

"Don't worry, Augie. I owe that man my life. I'll do whatever it takes to make sure he does his job."

"I know you're eager to move out of your aunt's house, Boudreaux. There are some inexpensive apartments in town, but if you'd like, I could let you and Johnny live in one of the small cottages on the grounds. It's not much to look at, but it's free."

"Thanks," Boudreaux said. "That would help us out a lot."

Spring gave way to summer. It didn't take long for Boudreaux and Johnny to master the intricate details of golf course maintenance. They dug holes, planted and pruned shrubs and trees, pulled weeds, cut grass, and fertilized and mulched the lush fairways and greens. They learned to operate, maintain, and repair the various mowers, bulldozers, and grader. They loved every second of it. More importantly, they learned to live again.

Before long, they could identify the myriad insects, birds, and other wildlife that inhabited the golf course. The wondrous signs of Mother Nature that surrounded them constantly amazed them. They also came to realize that sometimes a man has to lose everything except his faith and hope in order to appreciate the precious gift of life that God has given him.

One warm and pleasant evening, Boudreaux and Johnny lay on their backs on the edge of the eighteenth green. Johnny reached over and plucked a dandelion from the first cut next to him. "Know what this fuzzy-headed plant is called, Boudreaux?"

"It looks like a dandelion to me."

"Well, yeah. That's what it's called now. But a year ago, it would have been called 'lunch.'"

With that, he popped it in his mouth and started chewing. After a few seconds, Johnny made a face and spat out a spray of white particles. "It still tastes like crap."

Simultaneously, they both rolled back and forth with uncontrollable laughter.

Boudreaux leaned over on one elbow and smiled at his best friend. "You know, Johnny, I believe that's the first time we've had a good laugh since we got back."

"Yeah, you're right. I'd forgotten what it even felt like to laugh."

"Do you ever think about those days anymore, Johnny?"

"Every single day, Boudreaux. Every single day."

Boudreaux watched a hawk making lazy spirals above the swaying treetops. "I think we're both going to be just fine, Johnny. Just fine."

A few days later, an elderly club member, upset with his round, walked up on Boudreaux and Johnny digging up some dead Japanese boxwoods. They were laughing and throwing dirt clods at each other.

"Don't you boys ever have a bad day?" the man asked.

"Not anymore, sir," Boudreaux answered thoughtfully, rubbing his muddy hands on his overalls. "Not after what we went through. As far as I'm concerned, and I'm sure Johnny would agree with me, we'll never have another bad day for as long as we live."

As if to punctuate that last sentiment, a large chunk of mud smacked into the back of Boudreaux's head. Turning, Boudreaux scooped up a handful of mud and chased his cackling friend down the fairway, yelling, "You're dead meat, Johnny!"

The club member smiled and headed for the nineteenth hole for a stiff drink. "What a couple of screwballs," he muttered. Had he known the whole story of their ordeal during the war, he undoubtedly would have felt a deeper appreciation of his own privileged life.

Chapter Eight

Augie, Johnny, and Boudreaux formed that rare kind of bond that only combat veterans share. They spent many evenings enjoying each other's company, drinking whiskey, and swapping war stories. Augie's ability to remain silent and listen to his young friends did much to help them cope with their past. His compassionate nature made him more of a father figure than an employer.

Boudreaux noticed that Augie was a packrat; his office was cluttered and in a constant state of disarray. The small room adjoining Augie's office, at first glance, looked like any ordinary, packed storage locker. Since Augie gave Boudreaux and Johnny free rein to enter his office, Boudreaux decided one day to check out this back room. What greeted his eyes left him in total awe.

Hundreds of old photographs and newspaper clippings covered the walls. The photographs depicted mostly golfers and golf courses. He recognized the names of most of the American courses, but he'd never heard of many of the British and Scottish courses.

Trophies, plaques, and medals bore *Augie Henderson* engraved in fancy script. What captured his attention the most was shelf after shelf of assorted antique clubs, golf bags, balls, and tees. Neat, handwritten placards accompanied each item, giving their names, descriptions, and dates when they were used. This collection looked nothing like the equipment used in the modern golfing world.

The clubs had unusual names like mashie, spoon, niblick, brassie, and cleek. The collection of balls was even more mystifying with names like feathery (a dried leather pouch stuffed with compressed goose feathers), gutta-percha, and Haskell. A hickory-shafted, sheepskin-gripped enigma with an odd-looking blade caught Boudreaux's eye. The hosel had a small lever protruding from the back. With gradation lines etched into the blade, it appeared to be some sort of a mechanical device. *Darnedest thing I've ever seen,* Boudreaux thought, scratching his head. *I wonder what it's for.*

Augie didn't talk much about his past. All Boudreaux knew was he had emigrated from England as a young man. Glancing around the room, Boudreaux realized Augie must have had quite a golf career before settling at Whispering Hollows.

This isn't a storeroom, Boudreaux thought. *This is a golf museum.*

"Quite a sight, isn't it?" Augie whispered behind a startled Boudreaux. "Sorry, I didn't mean to scare you. You were so engrossed in your discovery I didn't want to disturb you."

"This is quite a collection you have here, Augie. How long have you been collecting this stuff?"

"That stuff, as you call it, was my life once upon a time. I say was because it's all in my past. I wasn't always a greenskeeper. After the Great War, I came home to Portsmouth, England, and discovered the grand old game of golf. Like you and Johnny, I needed to escape and find myself. I was a total wreck. I found that walking the links alone eased my mind and gave me a sense of peace."

Boudreaux leaned against the doorjamb as Augie continued his story.

"I got a job at a golf course and did odd jobs and caddied occasionally. I fell in love with the solitary lifestyle of the sport. I could enjoy the great outdoors with God and Mother Nature as my sole companions.

"When I wasn't working or playing, I found solace in scouring the pro shops from Portsmouth to Edinburgh, Scotland, collecting anything that had to do with golf. I also did a lot of thinking about my lot in life and asked God why he spared me and let so many of my friends die. I was thankful and angry at the same time. I was confused."

Boudreaux nodded. "I feel the same way sometimes, Augie. You think maybe God has special plans for us?"

"It's probably too late for me, but it's possible God did spare you for a reason, Boudreaux." Augie ran his fingers along his collection of clubs. "You just need to discover what that reason is."

"From the looks of those awards, you must have been quite a player," Boudreaux said with more than a trace of awe in his voice.

Augie slowly circled the room and looked around at the assorted reminders of a once-promising golf career.

"By 1920, I had become quite an accomplished amateur. I competed against the best players in England, Scotland, and America. With the encouragement of fellow golfers and employers, I turned professional in 1923, two years after marrying my childhood sweetheart."

Boudreaux detected a sadness in Augie's voice. "I heard it wasn't easy in those days."

"It was a real struggle, and it wasn't just the fact that pro golf didn't pay that well. Pros were considered second-class citizens in the community. Many looked on us as bums who couldn't hold down a regular job."

"How did your wife feel about your choice of profession?"

"She wasn't crazy about it, but she stuck by my side. She knew how important it was to me."

"What was it like, traveling around the country and visiting all the great courses?"

"During tournaments at ritzy golf clubs, we weren't even allowed to use members' clubhouses to change into our golfing duds. We had to change in the pro shops."

Augie led Boureaux back to his office, where he reached behind his desk and pulled out the bottle of whiskey and two glasses. He poured them both a drink.

"Thank God for your Walter Hagen. That American dynamo had guts—and style. I first saw him at the Open in 1920. That was the year it was held in Deal, a wee town on the English Channel. The American golfers, as well as a few of the British golfers, were complaining about having to change in the pro shop."

"I heard of him. He was one of my dad's idols."

"I happened to be standing by the members' clubhouse entrance trying to get a glimpse of some of the more famous golfers, when a beautiful black limousine pulled up and stopped ten feet away. The impeccably dressed driver opened the passenger door, and Hagen climbed out. He had a bottle of champagne and a glass in one hand and his shoes in the other. He waved and smiled confidently at the assembled crowd, then proceeded to pour himself a glass of the bubbly. After proposing a toast to the beautiful country and people of England, he sat on the limo's running board and changed into his golf shoes."

Augie walked over to the window and looked out over the golf course. He took a sip of his drink.

"The crowd went crazy," Augie said. "Amid cheers and applause and enthusiastic pats on the back, this larger-than-life character sauntered over to the first tee. Believe me, the hoity-toity club members were none too pleased with this spectacle."

Augie paused long enough to refill their glasses. "The press had a field day with that irreverent, thumb-of-the-nose at the pompous, elite club members. That small act of defiance set in motion the downfall of the discrimination pros had dealt with for years and did wonders to elevate their status."

Augie raised his glass. "A toast to Sir Walter. That was the day I knew the golfing life was meant for me. That man had life by the tail, and I wanted to be just like him."

"What happened after that?" Boudreaux asked.

"I continued to practice and play in as many tournaments as my busy work schedule would allow. As I mentioned, I played the best and managed to hold my own. I soon found out that America was where I needed to be. The game pretty much originated in Great Britain, but it was becoming more and more popular here. The American golfers told me professionals were treated with a little more respect here than in my country. That was all I needed to hear.

"After three more years of bouncing from tournament to tournament, I brought my wife and baby daughter to America. This was 1923. Golfing conditions in England were improving, but it appeared golf was coming close to surpassing baseball as America's favorite pastime. We settled in upstate New York. I took a job in a small golf resort in the Catskills but struggled with my dream of making a living as a professional. For the next five years, I worked on improving my game. My big break came when I qualified for the 1929 United States Open."

Augie fell silent as his face clouded over. He took a long drink of his whiskey as tears welled in his eyes. After a few moments of awkward silence, Boudreaux placed a hand on Augie's trembling shoulder.

"What happened, Augie?" Boudreaux gently asked, suspecting he wasn't going to like the answer.

"We were driving to the Tournament in Mamaroneck, just outside New York City. It was raining hard, and we were running late. I misjudged a curve and lost control of the car. We slid down a steep embankment and flipped over. I was knocked unconscious for several minutes, and, when I came to, I saw my wife lying in the wet grass. She had been thrown from the car. She was pretty banged up and barely alive. My little girl was pinned under the car. I managed to pull her free, but her left arm was badly mangled. She was only seven years old.

"An ambulance took us to a nearby hospital. I barely had a scratch. My wife died that night before I had a chance to tell her how much I loved and needed her. My daughter lost part of her arm just below the elbow, but the doctors said she would recover. Tell me, how does a little kid recover from something like that?"

"I'm sorry, Augie," Boudreaux said. "Where is your daughter now?"

"You might have seen her. She's a waitress in the club grill."

Boudreaux and Johnny couldn't very often afford to eat in the pricey Whispering Hollows Grill, but Boudreaux vaguely remembered seeing a young, petite, very attractive blonde girl waiting tables. Her name tag read *Jane*. He hadn't noticed her physical flaw, because she always had a towel draped over her left arm. Her imperfection didn't appear to dampen her job performance or her attitude and enthusiasm. She always wore a cheery smile and wasn't afraid to mingle with the customers. Boudreaux also remembered seeing an energetic, little tow-headed boy hanging around behind the counter.

"I didn't know she was your, daughter, Augie. I like her. It looks like you did a great job of raising her by yourself."

"I guess I did all right, but, the truth is, she took more care of me than I did of her. There were days I wanted to end it all, but sensing my sadness, she would jump in my lap, give me a big hug, and tell me not to worry, that she would always take care of her daddy.

"She's fiercely independent. She had to be. As a kid, she put up with a lot of cruel teasing. That pretty much stopped one day on the playground, when she flattened the school bully twice her size with a right cross. That was when I knew she would be all right. Lord help the man who ever treats her like a helpless invalid."

Boudreaux was a little reluctant to push Augie, since it was obviously a sensitive topic, but his curiosity got the better of him. "What happened after the accident?"

"This happened," Augie said, holding up the whiskey bottle. "I hardly touch the stuff anymore except on special occasions, but after the accident, I traded the hole in the green for the tiny hole in the top of the nearest bottle of booze."

Boudreaux nodded without saying a word. He didn't want to pry into Augie's personal business. He could see he was still hurting.

After a few moments, Augie stood and walked around the room, looking at the hundreds of keepsakes that reminded him of the past.

"I quit playing. I blamed myself for what happened to my wife and daughter. I was in such a fool hurry to get to the tournament that I became careless. I never lost my love for the game. To an extent, it did save my life. I just decided to put the game aside for a while. At least until the painful memories died down a little.

"I continued to work at the course in the Catskills, but a few months later, I decided I needed to get away. I didn't know where to go, so I just packed up my daughter, loaded all our personal belongings and my golf memorabilia into a small utility trailer, and headed west. I had no idea where we would end up."

Augie waved a hand at the storage room. "I didn't know if or when I'd play golf again, but as you can see, I wasn't ready to part with my memories.

"I made it to the middle of Texas when my car broke down. I had it towed to the nearest town, which happened to be the quaint little town of Kerrville. I liked what I saw, and when I discovered it had a small golf course, I decided to apply for a job there. The Whispering Hollows Country Club was nestled among the rolling hills of the Hill

Country. Fortunately, they needed an experienced assistant greenskeeper, and I was able to start immediately. It turned out to be a wise decision. Jane grew up here, and she loves the Hill Country as much as I do."

"Ever pick up your clubs again?" Boudreaux asked.

"No. I stored them in a box in the closet, where they'll stay until I feel the time is right to take them out again. The only clubs I touch now are the ones the club members need cleaned and repaired. Boudreaux, I've got everything I need. I have absolutely no desire to pick up my clubs right now. They'll still be there when I'm ready."

Boudreaux turned at the sound of running footsteps coming from the hallway. A few seconds later, a young blond-haired boy burst through the door and made a beeline to Augie.

"Grandpa, let's go fishing," he said. "You promised."

"Boudreaux, meet my grandson, Mickey," Augie said, rubbing the boy's hair affectionately. "Mickey, this here is my friend, Boudreaux."

"Hi, Boudreaux," Mickey said, flashing a broad grin as he took his grandpa's hand. "That's a funny name. I'm five years old."

"Hi, Mickey," Boudreaux said, as he leaned over to tousle Mickey's mop of unruly hair. "Yeah, I guess it is a funny name." He laughed.

Mickey quickly turned his attention back to Augie. "Come on, Grandpa. Let's go."

"Later, Mickey. Boudreaux and I are talking right now. You run along now. I promise you those big old catfish will still be waiting for us."

Mickey frowned with disappointment and ran out the door.

"Nice-looking kid, Augie. I didn't even know Jane was married and that you were a grandfather."

"She's not married anymore. Back in '40, a nice-looking, young Army soldier on a weekend furlough from San Antonio dropped by with some buddies. His name was George Beck. They met in the grill and took a shine to each other. It was a credit to his character that her little imperfection didn't bother him in the least.

"A few months later they got married and moved to San Antonio. That was really tough on me to see her go. A year later, Mickey was born. They were the only family I had. When Germany declared war on the United States, George was immediately sent to England. It nearly broke Jane's heart when a couple of officers and a chaplain showed up at her door and informed her George had been killed in action in the summer of '43. It happened during the Allied invasion of Sicily. Jane and Mickey came back here to live with me. Unfortunately, Mickey was too young to remember his father. I guess I've been more of a father to him than a grandfather."

"They're both lucky to have you, Augie."

"Not as lucky as I am to have them," Augie replied. "By the way, how's Johnny doing? I remember, for a while there, he was having some problems adjusting to being home."

"After that first couple of flashbacks, he seemed to be doing fine. I figured with time, he would get back to his old self, but last night he had another episode."

"Jeez, another one? I really feel for him, Boudreaux. When I came home from Europe, I had some scary episodes myself. Back then they just called it shell shock. I don't know what they call it now. I had some terrible memories of the terrible things I witnessed. And it wasn't just the bombs and the bullets—the Germans had a new weapon. It was called mustard gas. It burned your lungs and blinded you. I managed to avoid the worst of it. Just stick by Johnny's side, Boudreaux. That's about all you can do to help him right now."

"Thanks for the drink, Augie. I'd better get back and check on Johnny."

Boudreaux returned to his cabin and cautiously opened the front door. He found Johnny sitting on the living room floor with his back against the wall. His arms were tightly grasped around his knees, and his vacant eyes were fixed on the opposite wall.

"Hi, Johnny."

"Hi, Boudreaux."

"You okay, Johnny? You want me to fix you something to eat?"

"Nah. I'm not hungry. I just want to sit here a while. Sorry to be such a pain in the neck. When is it ever going to end, Boudreaux?"

"I don't know, but we'll get through this together. You want to see the doc again?"

"No. I can't stomach any more of his stupid questions. They just make me feel worse."

"We went through an awful lot, Johnny. The doc warned us it might take a long time to get a grip on things."

"How about you, Boudreaux? You doing okay? You scared the heck out of me and half the customers at that restaurant. I thought the cops were going to arrest you."

Johnny wasn't the only one having trouble with his post-war ordeal. Halfway through their dinner at a Chinese restaurant the previous week, a waiter dropped a large serving bowl of rice near their table. The loud crash of the shattering china startled Boudreaux, and for a few moments, Boudreaux had a vivid flashback: He was back at Camp Fukuoka #17. As were all his fellow POWs, he was starving and suffering from severe malnutrition.

One of the guards maliciously dropped a wooden bucket of maggot-infested, boiled rice on the dirt floor in front of Boudreaux and the other prisoners. "Din-air ees served, janter-man," the guard cackled in his thick Japanese accent. The starving men ignored the insult and dove at the mess on the floor, frantically stuffing handfuls of the soiled, sticky globs of rice into their mouths. Having lost all vestiges of civilized, human behavior, they elbowed, shoved, and punched each other to fill their aching stomachs.

When Boudreaux snapped back to reality, he was on the restaurant floor, his mouth stuffed with rice and his hands scratching frantically at the gleaming tile, greedily searching for every morsel he could recover. The manager had called the police, but Johnny did some fast talking that kept Boudreaux from being taken away to jail. Thankfully, one of the policemen was a World War II vet and sympathized with Boudreaux's plight. Feeling a deep sense of embarrassment and shame at his behavior, Boudreaux was reluctant to go out in public for a while.

"That was some night, wasn't it?" Boudreaux said. "I think I'd better avoid that place for a while."

"We're quite a pair, aren't we, Boudreaux?"

"We'll be all right, Johnny. We just need to stick together."

"Boudreaux, during the flight back from Japan, you were mumbling something about having big plans for the two of us."

"You remember my saying that? I was just talking to myself. I thought you were asleep."

"I was dozing on and off. I was still having some pretty bad headaches, and that medicine the doc gave me wouldn't let me get a good night's sleep. What big plans were you talking about?"

"Maybe it's just a pipe dream, but do you remember my talking about golfing with my dad?"

"Yeah, I remember. You said those were your happiest days."

"My dad said I had a natural golfing touch. He told me professional golf was big in Great Britain and was getting more and more popular in America. He thought that if I really worked at it, I might be able to make a decent living at it. The prize purses weren't that big yet, but some of the better professionals picked up a lot of extra cash doing exhibitions."

"That's great for you, but how do I fit in?"

"A golf pro needs a caddie. That's where you come in. I could teach you everything you need to know. The great thing is we wouldn't be punching a clock for some slave driver. Also, we would get to work in the great outdoors."

"I don't know, Boudreaux. You know my left arm and leg don't work too well, anymore. I doubt if I could carry your clubs around a golf course."

"Don't worry about that right now," Boudreaux said, as he put his arm around Johnny's shoulder, nursing a gut feeling that Johnny might be right. He remembered the promise he had made to himself—he would do whatever it took to take care of Johnny. He aimed to keep that promise. "I feel God spared both of us for a reason. I'll figure something out."

Boudreaux and Johnny continued working at Whispering Hollows Country Club, and, by the summer of 1947, the memories of the horrors of their past as well as the frightening flashbacks had subsided considerably. The close buddies kept busy and did their best with what God had left them with: their freedom, companionship, hope for the future, and especially their appreciation for living in such a great country that so many of their comrades had died to protect.

Johnny, with occasional help from Boudreaux, managed to keep up with the physical demands of the job. In his free time, Boudreaux visited the driving range and pounded balls using a beat-up set of used clubs he found in the maintenance shed. He spent hours hitting hundreds of balls, long after the range lights had been extinguished.

With the same clubs, he roamed the course in the morning before it opened to members and stayed long after it closed at night, until he could barely see, hitting every conceivable shot imaginable. He practiced hitting from grass, dirt, mud, and caliche rock. He learned to control ball trajectories from uphill, downhill, and sidehill lies. He mastered the ability to hit balls high and low at will. He learned to fade and draw his shots.

More importantly, he learned the importance of imagining the outcome of every shot in his head before addressing the ball and then executing the shot as planned. At times, he felt as if he and the ball had become one. His confidence soared. Many evenings, he returned to his cabin with blistered and bleeding hands from hitting so many balls.

"Johnny, I think I'm on a first-name-basis with every tree, bush, and rock on this course," Boudreaux said after a particularly tough practice session. He grimaced as Johnny carefully applied first aid salve to his sore hands.

"How's your game coming along?" Johnny asked.

"Not bad," Boudreaux said. "The flexibility in my left wrist isn't too good. I can thank Funaki for that." Boudreaux's body had healed from the beatings at the hand of the camp commander, but his broken left wrist hadn't healed properly, leaving him unable to flex it properly. Fortunately, Boudreaux had learned to compensate for it with his stiff, unorthodox swing.

"I'm hitting them long and straight. I can shape my shots to curve the ball left and right when I need to. The hours I've spent on the putting green are paying off. I know I can take most of the arrogant duffers in the club."

"Has anyone seen you play yet?"

"Not many. I try not to practice when anyone's watching. I want to wait and catch everyone by surprise."

"And when will that be? You're out there every day tearing up the course when no one's watching. You think you can keep that up in front of others?"

"We'll find out next month, Johnny. I entered the Fourth of July Club Championship. It will just be one round. It's supposed to be for members only, but Augie appealed to the owner's patriotism to get me a special invitation. Oh, by the way, you'll be caddying for me."

"I can try, Boudreaux, but I don't know if I'll last the whole round."

"You won't know until you try."

Boudreaux continued to work on his game in his spare time. He felt he was ready to take on anybody. The day of the tournament, Boudreaux showed up full of confidence despite an initial case of the jitters. Johnny was a nervous wreck but vowed to do his best to keep up.

Boudreaux started out hitting some careless shots, but when the excitement wore off, he settled down to business. By the end of the round, he had waxed the living daylights out of the other golfers, winning by a large margin. The only blemish on his round was that he had to carry his clubs on the back nine. Johnny could walk the course on his own, but carrying the heavy bag full of clubs and other gear proved to be too much. His positive attitude and desire to complete the task just weren't enough. Boudreaux was dismayed but wasn't about to give up on his friend.

"Sorry, Boudreaux," a dejected Johnny said. "Congratulations on your win, but I think I was more of a burden than a help out there."

"Don't ever say that, Johnny. You'll never be a burden to me. I wouldn't even be here if it wasn't for you. We'll figure something out. You're still my caddie, and I already told you I'm not doing this without you."

Boudreaux didn't have the heart to mention it to Johnny, but, after the round, several club members, upon learning of Boudreaux's professional golf aspirations, advised him to dump Johnny and get a real caddie. Boudreaux lost his temper and almost struck one of the men.

"Nobody touches Johnny!" He growled at the shocked men before storming away.

They don't understand, he thought, as he slammed his clubs to the ground and sat on a bench by the driving range. He held his head in his hands and wept. *They'll never understand.*

Chapter Nine

"Hit it, you big ape."

The squeaky voice could barely be heard from behind the practice tees. Boudreaux paused and glanced at Johnny out of the corner of his eye. He re-gripped his club and kept his stance over the ball motionless.

"Where's that sneaky little monkey this time?" he whispered.

"He's hiding behind the water cooler," Johnny said under his breath. "That moron thinks we won't see him there."

Boudreaux shook his head and laughed. "Don't let on that we know he's there. Just follow my lead."

"You got it. Let the fun begin."

"Gee, Johnny," Boudreaux said in a loud, puzzled voice. "I must be going crazy. I swear there's a ghost in those woods talking to me."

"Aw, that's just your imagination," Johnny said, trying to keep a straight face.

"Hey, Mr. Ghost, are you talking to me?" Boudreaux drawled in a meek voice. "Please don't scare me while I'm trying to hit my golf ball."

"Yeah, I'm talking to you, you idiotic space worm," said the tiny voice coming from behind the water cooler, followed by muffled giggling.

"Oooh, Johnny! We better get out of here before something terrible happens."

Boudreaux flashed three fingers at Johnny and cocked his head in the direction of the cooler. "One...two...three," he whispered. After the final count, Boudreaux dropped his club and, simultaneously, he and Johnny rushed the water cooler, Boudreaux dashing around the right side and Johnny around the left. Boudreaux grabbed the squirming boy's arms, and Johnny grabbed his flailing legs.

"Well, lookee here, Boudreaux. It's our ghost. What should we do to teach him a lesson this time? I say we toss him in the creek."

"Nah, that's too good for him," Boudreaux said. "Besides, his stinky feet would probably kill all the fish. I think we should throw him in that patch of prickly pear cactus. That'll keep him out of our hair for a while. Maybe then I'll be able to practice my swing in peace."

"Excellent idea, Boudreaux."

Boudreaux and Johnny dragged the kicking and screaming boy over to the edge of the cactus and swung him back and forth a few times.

"On the count of three, Johnny. Ready? One, two—"

"When you two numbskulls are done torturing my son, you think you could give me a hand with the grill?" asked a young woman, feigning exasperation. She wore a greasy apron and twirled a pair of tongs in her right hand. "These hot dogs aren't going to cook themselves."

Boudreaux and Johnny dropped the relieved, six-year-old Mickey on the ground and hustled over to the picnic table adjoining the golf course's driving range.

"Your wish is our command," Boudreaux said in a passable English accent while bowing graciously at the waist.

Jane rolled her eyes and told Mickey to be sure to wash his hands.

"Uncle Boudreaux," Mickey asked. "Were you and Uncle Johnny really going to throw me in that cactus?"

Boudreaux answered, "Mickey, you're just lucky your mom showed up when she did."

"Yeah," Augie added, laughing. "Or you might have been the only kid in second grade who looked like a pin cushion."

Jane gave Mickey an affectionate hug. "Good thing I stopped them. How would I ever be able to do this again if you had all those sharp needles poking out everywhere?"

"Aw, Mom!" Mickey said, with his crooked gap-toothed grin.

Over the past year, Boudreaux and Johnny had wormed their way into the hearts of Augie and his family, especially little Mickey. They saw a lot of themselves in his mischievous antics and took it upon themselves to be surrogate fathers to a little boy who desperately needed a man's influence and guidance.

Through one of life's cruel fates, Mickey never got to know his real father. Jane showered him with love and affection and had done a fine job of raising him, but he needed someone to take him fishing and hunting. Someone to teach him how to become a man. Augie had tried to fill that role, but, at his age, didn't quite have the energy to keep up with a growing, rambunctious boy. Also, his greenskeeping duties didn't allow him much free time to spend with Mickey. Boudreaux and Johnny loved the boy as if he were their own flesh and blood, and they were determined to help Jane with his rearing any way they could.

After lunch, Boudreaux and Johnny helped Jane clean up around the grill and picnic table. The three of them then joined Augie and Mickey on the soft grass of the driving range a few yards away. For several minutes, they sat without saying a word, enjoying each other's company.

"Uncle Boudreaux," Mickey said, breaking the silence. "How come you're always out here practicing your golf? Don't you ever get bored?"

Mickey was referring to Boudreaux's obsessive presence on the course or the driving range, where he spent nearly all his free time hitting balls or studying the varying conditions of the course. He analyzed the effects of wind, rain, and drought on his shots. He got down on his knees and evaluated the grains of the different grasses to better understand the physics of hitting a ball. He sometimes exhibited a madman's determination to master every aspect of this wonderful, intoxicating game.

"How could I ever get bored doing something I love? Especially when, while doing it, I get to look at God's beautiful handiwork? See all those tall trees lining the fairway? Those beautiful clouds in the sky? The green grass and the magnificent creatures that roam through these woods?"

Boudreaux put his arm around the young boy's shoulder and squeezed. "You see, Mickey, there was a time when I thought I'd never get the chance to see those things again. When you come close to losing all that, it does something to you. I guess you could say God gave me a second chance, and I'm not going to let Him down. No sir, I could stand here and look at this all day long and never get bored."

Mickey looked off in the distance as if contemplating what Boudreaux had just said. He then turned to Johnny. "Uncle Johnny, I got a question for you," he asked with a serious look on his face.

"Fire away, little man," Johnny said, wondering what profound query was to follow.

"What would you do if a girl kissed you?"

Johnny exchanged quizzical glances with Boudreaux, Jane, and Augie. For a moment, he was at a loss for words. Finally, he regained his composure.

"Uh...well..." He looked to Boudreaux, who responded with a shrug and a raised eyebrow.

"Well, what would you do?" Boudreaux asked, with an eager look on his face. "I'd like to know, too."

Johnny's expression suddenly changed from bewilderment to sly mischief. He dramatically rubbed his chin with feigned seriousness.

"Why, I'd rip her lips off and tie them in a knot around her head," Johnny said.

Mickey rolled over on his back, laughing hysterically for a few seconds, then bolted upright. "And then what would you do?"

"Why, I'd grab a handful of peanuts and stuff them up her nose."

Again, Mickey was overcome with uncontrollable laughter and rolled back and forth on the grass. "And then what would you do?"

"Why, I'd grab a banana and—"

"Enough already!" Jane shouted, trying to look serious but failing badly. "Johnny, how about you let me teach Mickey about the birds and the bees? If he listens to any more of your nonsense, he'll end up more of a mess than he already is. Mickey, why would you even ask your Uncle Johnny such a silly question?"

"Yesterday, a girl in my class dragged me into a closet and kissed me on the lips. It was yucky."

Boudreaux leaned over to Jane. "Maybe you should start planning that birds and bees talk soon," he whispered. "I hear those closets can be downright dangerous places to be."

"Sometimes, I think you and Johnny are both nuts," Jane said with a smirk, as she stood up and herded Mickey back to their cabin. "But, you're lovable nuts," she added with a smile as she looked back over her shoulder.

Augie, Boudreaux, and Johnny remained sitting on the grass, quietly enjoying the balmy evening and watching the sun set over the darkening, rolling hills of the Whispering Hollows Golf Course. After dusk settled over the course and the lengthening shadows of the trees snaked across the fairways, Johnny stood, stretched, and yawned.

"Sorry to leave you gents," he said. "But I believe I'll turn in early. Dragging them fertilizer bags around all day has left me plum tuckered out. Goodnight, all."

"Goodnight, Johnny," Boudreaux and Augie said in unison.

After a few minutes, Augie turned to Boudreaux. "How's Johnny doing?"

"He seems to be doing all right. He hasn't complained of any flashbacks lately. That's a good sign. In fact, I haven't had any in almost a year. I think the worst is behind us."

"I can see he's getting stronger, but I've noticed his left arm and left leg are still giving him trouble. What did the doc say about that?"

Boudreaux frowned. "He said the nerve damage is probably permanent. He can adapt to an extent, but he'll always have trouble carrying heavy loads for more than short periods. Which brings me to a big concern I have."

"It's his ability to caddie, isn't it?"

"Yeah. This past year, my game has improved considerably. You've seen the trophies I've brought home from those amateur events from around the state."

"I've seen them. I don't know what's piqued the interest of the fans and officials more. Your uncanny finesse and domination of the course or the fact that you refuse to hire a caddie and always insist on carrying your own clubs."

"Years ago, I made a promise to Johnny that he would be the only caddie I'll ever use. Until that day comes, I'll carry the bag myself. I plan on going pro some day and, if it comes to it, I may be the only golfer out there carrying his own bag." Boudreaux laughed. "I still don't know if that's even allowed."

"I don't see why not," Augie said. "What does Johnny have to say about all this?"

"He thinks I'm making a mistake. Says I should forget about my promise to him and just do what I need to do to succeed. He feels carrying my own bag would interfere with my game. He's probably right, but I don't care. I told him it will be him or it will be no one."

"Have you thought about using a lightweight bag and just a few clubs? He might be able to handle that for eighteen holes."

"We tried that, but he still had trouble completing the whole round. Besides, I can't compete effectively without a full set of clubs. Those other players are just too good. Augie, I need him out there with me, but more importantly, he needs to be out there for himself. Right now, he feels like he's failed me. That after all the plans we made, he's let me down. Can you believe that? I owe that man so much, Augie. There's got to be a way to get him out there on the course with me."

In the deepening twilight, Augie could barely make out Boudreaux's face, but he could see the glistening reflection of light in his eyes as tears slowly formed and ran down his cheeks.

Augie rose to his feet and paced back and forth for a few minutes, mumbling to himself. He finally stopped, snapped his fingers as if struck with divine inspiration, then came over and sat next to Boudreaux.

"It's a long shot, Boudreaux, but I think I may have a solution to your problem."

Boudreaux looked at Augie with a slight ray of hope. "If you have a solution to this problem, Augie, you're a miracle worker."

"Come by my office first thing in the morning. I want to show you something. Don't say anything to Johnny yet. I don't want to get his hopes up until you and I are sure my idea will work. It's time for me to head home, Boudreaux. I'll see you in the morning."

"Thanks, Augie. See you tomorrow."

Boudreaux showed up at Augie's office at the crack of dawn, eager to find out what he had up his sleeve. Augie ushered him back to his storeroom and retrieved one of his prize artifacts from its place on the wall.

"Boudreaux, you once commented on this odd-looking club. You said it looked like some sort of measuring device."

"Yeah, I was wondering about those funny-looking lines etched into the metal and that lever in the back. It kind of looks like a futuristic golf club."

"You're partially right, except your timeline is off a bit. In the late 1800s, several golf club makers experimented with something called an adjustable golf club. Various designs were considered, all centering around the novel idea of using one club for all a player's shot-making needs. All clubs, from the 1 iron through the sand wedge, including the woods and putter, have club faces with varying degrees of loft.

"Why not, the club makers proposed, apply modern technology to build one club with an adjustable face that can be rotated to the desired angle? That way, a golfer would be liberated from having to lug a heavy set of clubs around the golf course. He wouldn't necessarily need a hire a caddie unless one was needed to give advice or offer moral support."

"That does make sense," Boudreaux said. "But why aren't they used today?"

"Many club makers came up with functioning proto-types, but all faced four major obstacles. One—even though the desired club face angle was easy to achieve, the changing position of the leading edge of the blade in relation to the shaft made consistent ball contact difficult to control, even for professionals. Two—the blade wasn't as big and heavy as the heads on the woods, restricting the distance a ball could be hit. That, alone, dissuaded the long-hitters. Three—most people thought it was a short-lived, ridiculous-looking gimmick or fad that would eventually fade in popularity. Imagine how the other golfers and fans would react watching a player pull out a wrench or other adjusting tool every time he needed to change the angle of his club. Four—traditionalists were dead set against it because they felt it violated the very spirit of the game."

"Let me see that thing." Boudreaux said. He took it from Augie and closely examined the small lever on the back of the club head. Augie explained that by pushing it in and pulling out the spring-loaded blade, one could rotate the blade to the desired angle of loft. "Wow! That's ingenious, yet it looks simple enough to use. Apparently, this particular design doesn't need an adjusting tool."

"There were many different configurations. I've seen a few, but most people I talked to said this design was the most successful, since it was the easiest to use. Not enough to gain popular approval, but enough to be taken seriously."

Boudreaux turned the club over in his hands and noticed the word *Urquhart* stamped on the back. "Is this the name of the man who designed it?"

"It is. Robert Urquhart and his wife, Edith, had several patents on different clubs. This particular one was patented in 1905."

"Where did you get it?" Boudreaux asked.

"I met Robert in 1921 in Edinburgh, Scotland. I was at the top of my game, and he and I were fortunately set up by mutual friends in a friendly match. He was quite an amateur himself—and very competitive. He was a gambling man, and, unfortunately for him, his bravado was larger than his purse. After nine holes, I was trouncing him to the tune of twenty pounds. He insisted on doubling the stakes on the back nine but couldn't catch me.

"When I requested my winnings, he said I would have to wait a few days for him to collect such a large sum. He did, however, make me an unusual offer. He asked me if I would accept his prototype adjustable club in lieu of the money. Suspecting I would probably never see him or the money after the round, I accepted his offer.

"I tried to make a go of it, but I could never manage to hit the thing. I finally just figured it would make an interesting addition to my growing golf memorabilia collection. People get a laugh out of it when I show it to them. Why don't you take it and see if you can do something with it? If you can tame it, it may be Johnny's ticket back onto the course. He shouldn't have too much trouble carrying that club and a few extra balls and tees in his pocket."

"Thanks, Augie. We may be onto something here. And don't worry about me mastering this club. It looks like it may be my only chance to fulfill my promise to Johnny. I can promise you, I'll do whatever it takes to learn to hit this crazy-looking thing."

After thanking him again, Boudreaux walked out of Augie's office, reverently cradling the possible solution to the problem that had been plaguing him for the past year. A grin spread across his face. *Whatever it takes, old buddy. Whatever it takes. You and I are going to set the golf world on its ear.*

Chapter Ten

At three a.m. on a balmy, summer morning in 1947, the only sounds breaking the silence of the dark expanse of the forested Whispering Hollows Golf Course were the chirping of crickets and the occasional hoot of a barn owl. Only the natural nighttime sounds of nature, that is. Infringing on this soothing, nocturnal symphony came another sound, a mysterious clicking noise emanating from a cabin a few yards off the eighteenth fairway.

The light of the full moon lying low in the western sky silhouetted the figure of a man on the cabin's porch. His boyish face was illuminated by a single kerosene lamp hanging from a nail on a post by the front door. Alone in his thoughts, Boudreaux sat in his favorite chair, a rustic rocker he had fashioned from a large cedar that had succumbed to recent course renovations. His hands busily twisted and turned a curious-looking object made of metal and wood.

Incredible! Boudreaux thought, as he marveled at Robert Urquhart's adjustable club. He was fascinated, not only by its mechanics, but also by its simplicity. *Why hasn't anyone thought of using this before now? It can't be that hard to figure out. The sheepskin grip I can replace with a leather one. The hickory shaft is still in good condition. The adjustable head should be fine with a little oil and polishing. I believe I can make this work. I can't wait to take a crack at this.*

Boudreaux's calloused fingers explored the club's hosel and blade. Peering close, he wondered what the number "1445" stamped on the hosel signified. Beneath the numbers were the words "Urquhart Patent." The designer's name was also stamped on the face of the blade. Boudreaux pulled himself up from the chair and quietly tiptoed into the cabin.

"What are you up to?" a yawning Johnny asked. "You've been out there for hours. And what was that clicking noise? It sounded like you were cracking pecans."

"I was just doing some thinking," Boudreaux said. "I've come up with an idea."

"Aw, you're always coming up with crazy ideas. If you've discovered a way to turn manure and compost into gold, count me in. Otherwise, keep your thinking down so I can get some sleep."

Boudreaux laughed. "You're almost right, Johnny. Except, without the manure and compost, that is. I may have found a way to turn leather, iron, and wood into gold."

"Go to sleep, Boudreaux. You're not making any sense."

Johnny pulled his pillow over his face and soon added the sound of sawing logs to the night air. Boudreaux smiled affectionately at his sleeping friend. *I'm taking this thing to the top, and you're coming with me.* He carefully slid the club under his bed and hit the sack, his mind soon filled with dreams of smashing long drives and coaxing home difficult putts with his new wonder club, while the galleries went wild with cheers and applause. He also pictured his proud father looking down on him from Heaven above, cheering him on with a loving smile on his face.

Early the next morning, several hours before he started his maintenance duties, Boudreaux was on the driving range, hitting ball after ball with the new club. Augie was right. It was extremely hard to hit. *No wonder golfers gave up on it so quickly,* he thought. *They never really gave it a chance. But I'm not giving up. I'm going to hit this club until either I break or the club does.*

Boudreaux continued to practice hitting the club every chance he got. He tried to do so when no one, especially Johnny, was around. He realized how silly he must have looked out there, stopping every few minutes to adjust the club to a different loft setting. He wanted to make sure he got practice using every single blade position. He kept this activity from Johnny for the time being because he didn't want to get Johnny's hopes up, in case this experiment to master this club failed. When he felt total confidence in his swing, he would bring Johnny in.

He soon found out the biggest problem was the infernal variations of club face positions for each loft setting. The higher the loft, the further the leading edge of the club face jutted forward. That was something he could learn to cope with in time. Another problem was the lack of distance with the lower lofted settings. He would have to compensate for that with improved accuracy. That would take even more practice. Whatever amount of time the other golfers put into their practice sessions, he would double it for his sessions. *If I can't outdrive them, I'll just outwork them. Whatever it takes to beat them, I'll do it.*

By early fall, after several grueling months of intense practice and feeling he had achieved satisfactory control of his overall game, Boudreaux felt he was ready to show his hand to Johnny. Carrying the club, Boudreaux asked Johnny to join him sitting on the porch steps. Boudreaux handed the club to Johnny. With no small amount of curiosity, Johnny turned it over and over in his hands, listening intently as Boudreaux explained how the club worked.

"You're willing to sacrifice that much control and power using this club just to keep me out there as your caddie? You sure you want to do that?"

"The control will come with practice, Johnny. I'm giving up distance, but I'll more than make up for that with skill, finesse, and proper course management. Not to mention having a superior caddie in my corner."

Boudreaux gently laid his hand on Johnny's shoulder. "Don't worry. We can do this. Together. How many times do I have to tell you? It's always been you and me, and it will always be you and me. Got that?"

"Okay," Johnny said, with a slight smile spreading across his face. "But we're going to look pretty strange out there with everyone laughing, and you know they will be, while you're swinging that two-quart club and me carrying that goofy-looking thing in a three-foot-long sock slung over my shoulder."

Boudreaux laughed. "It's called an Urquhart club, not a two-quart club. And we'll ultimately be the one's laughing—all the way to the bank."

The next day, Boudreaux gave a demonstration of his shot-making skills to Augie, Jane, and Mickey. Augie's pride didn't mask the tears of joy in his eyes when he saw how Boudreaux had mastered his little novelty. Jane looked awestruck but was obviously pleased when she found out how Augie and Boudreaux had come up with a way to keep Johnny in the game. Mickey, on the other hand, couldn't stop laughing at the bizarre sight of Johnny's twisting and mashing the club head every time Boudreaux requested a different club.

"Keep laughing, little boy," Johnny said, as he took off running after a giggling Mickey. "I believe this club also has a special setting for spanking little boys."

After the demonstration, the five of them dropped by the grill to share a toast to the future of golf. The clinking of beer bottles (and one root beer bottle) could be heard above the din of the crowded room.

With Johnny loyally at his side, Boudreaux continued to practice with the Urquhart club, spending every available waking hour honing his golfing skills. Johnny became adept at adjusting the club's loft to meet the needs of every shot. He usually had it adjusted even before Boudreaux said anything. He seemed to have the uncanny ability to read Boudreaux's mind and, at times, appeared to know Boudreaux's game better than Boudreaux did himself. Furthermore, Johnny wasn't afraid to overrule Boudreaux's judgment on occasion, oftentimes resulting in heated words. They were a perfect match.

Occasionally, Augie joined them in their practice sessions. He mostly observed, but, when pressed, gave much-appreciated advice on swing mechanics as well as insight concerning the importance of the mind game. He reminded Boudreaux that his two most important pieces of equipment were the gray matter between his ears and that beautiful organ called a heart beating within his chest. Augie had, as both Boudreaux and Johnny knew, been there in the trenches, and his vast tournament experience complemented their zeal and enthusiasm.

Jane, not one to be left out, pitched in by bringing jugs of lemonade and sandwiches as well as moral support to the practice tees.

Mickey, in his own way, might have made the biggest sacrifice in helping his Uncle Boudreaux and Uncle Johnny. He volunteered to shag balls for Boudreaux in a nearby pasture when the driving range was full of club members. His job was to stand at the far end of the open field while Boudreaux pounded hundreds of golf balls in his direction. After Boudreaux hit all the balls, Mickey ran around the field and collected them in a canvas bag. He then ran back to Boudreaux and dumped the balls at his feet, after which he sprinted back out and resumed his position in the field, awaiting another barrage.

Mickey relished the chance to contribute to Boudreaux's training and to spend time with his uncles, though his propensity to daydream or poke sticks at fire ant mounds left him with more than a few knots on his head from not watching for incoming golf balls. Mickey didn't seem to mind, though. He proudly wore those bruises and lumps in much the same way a combat veteran brandished battle scars. He was just happy to be a part of Boudreaux's mission.

The new club caused quite a stir when Boudreaux began using it in public. That October, a charitable group was hosting a one-day amateur tournament in San Antonio at the small but challenging Brackenridge Golf Course. Claiming the distinction of being the oldest public golf course in Texas, it was one Boudreaux was very familiar with, having played there with or caddied for his dad many times.

The prize money wasn't much, but for Boudreaux, this was nothing more than a shakedown cruise. They wanted to see what kind of reaction they would get from tournament officials and fans in the gallery.

Prior to the tournament, word had spread through the golf community of central Texas about this unusual pair of combat veterans: Boudreaux making his debut with his peculiar-looking golf club and Johnny, his frail-looking, limping caddie carrying the club in a makeshift cloth bag. For that reason, the gallery was packed more with dubious curiosity-seekers than with actual golf fans. Some laughed when they saw Boudreaux's club for the first time.

Let them laugh, thought Boudreaux. *Let's see who's laughing when we take the prize money and the trophy home tonight.*

Boudreaux stood at the old limestone starter's shack, looking around and marveling at the beauty of the venerable course with its abundance of oak and pecan trees. He was suddenly overcome with emotion.

Hasn't changed much since I caddied for Dad all those years ago. I can still remember stuffing Dad's golf bag with pecans when he wasn't looking and that bag getting heavier and heavier as the round wore on. Boudreaux smiled. *I wonder what Dad would think if he could see me now.*

As Boudreaux walked over and teed up his ball on the first hole, he noticed the other three caddies, large, strapping jock-types staring contemptuously at Johnny and the empty golf bag slung over his shoulder. The larger of the three whispered something to the other two caddies, after which they all shook their heads and made no attempt to stifle their amusement.

Johnny was not one to take any baloney from anyone, least of all these smart alecks. He crossed the tee box and gave the one who'd whispered a steely eye.

"You find something funny, friend?" Johnny asked.

"Nah," the kid said with a smirk. Obviously, he figured this old geezer half his size wasn't much of a threat. "We just wondered how your guy expects to compete with that one sorry-looking excuse for a club."

"Well, you may be right," Johnny said with a slight smile. "But not to worry. If he starts losing, and I think he needs another club, I'll just borrow one of yours."

"Oh, yeah?" The kid said, closing the distance between himself and Johnny. He puffed out his already massive chest, as if expecting Johnny to be intimidated by such a pathetic display of machismo. "You think you're going to just borrow one of my clubs? Just like that?"

"Yeah. That's right. And if Boudreaux hits a good shot with it, I'll slide it gently back into your bag with much gratitude. And I might even slip you a nickel so you can buy yourself a lollipop." At that point, Johnny leaned in even closer, his penetrating eyes drilling holes in the kid's. "But you better pray that he hits a good shot with it, because if he flubs it up, I may just shove that club up your keester far enough to straighten that crooked nose of yours."

The kid froze, the fear evident in his eyes, which, by now, were the size of saucers. After the paralysis wore off, he lurched backward, crashing into the other caddies. All three of them fell to the ground with their golf bags, clubs, and balls spilling all over the tee box. Boudreaux's playing partners blew up and hurled a few choice obscenities at their caddies.

"What the heck's wrong with you clowns?" one screamed.

"You trying to ruin my new clubs?" another shouted.

"Who hired these idiots?" the third one added. "You guys better shape up or we'll get someone else."

Johnny looked over at Boudreaux with a smug grin and gave him a wink. "I believe you're up, partner."

Boudreaux scratched his head, wondering what Johnny had said to the other caddie to cause such a commotion. *Maybe it's best if I don't know,* he thought. He knew Johnny could sometimes be a live wire with a wicked sense of humor.

The other caddies never quite recovered their composure, and, for the remainder of the round, continued to make mistakes: handing out wrong clubs, losing balls, and leaving putters on previously played greens. The irritability of the other players grew as the round progressed.

While the other golfers in Boudreaux's foursome played horrendously, thanks in large part to the bumbling of their caddies, who appeared to be deathly afraid of this small, limping man with the icy stare, Boudreaux fired one of the best rounds of his life.

The only dark spot in an otherwise remarkable round occurred on the fourth hole. Boudreaux's drive hooked left, coming to rest in the rough a few feet from the cart path. He was left with a challenging, one-hundred-and-twenty-five-yard pitch shot to the green. A tall palm tree blocking his approach to the pin made the shot difficult. As he discussed his club selection with Johnny, a voice from the past, with a thick Japanese accent, sent a shiver down his spine.

"Budo, cafo of de pom."

As Boudreaux slowly turned toward the gallery to locate the source of this frightening voice, he noticed a look of fear in Johnny's eyes. He had heard it, too.

"No. It can't be him," Boudreaux muttered to Johnny. "Funaki can't be here, of all places. If it's him, I swear I'll kill him on the spot."

He scanned the faces of the group of spectators until his gaze settled on a small, middle-aged, Asian man wearing large round glasses and flashing a friendly smile.

"Cafo of de big pom tree. It brocks the green," the man said. "You must hit row shot to reach green. Everybody try go over. Cannot do. Secret is go under tree."

He looked Japanese to Boudreaux. If so, he was the first Japanese person Boudreaux had seen since returning from the war. Kneeling, Boudreaux tried to catch his breath. He felt a tightening in his chest. If he was Japanese, that would account for his pronouncing his name the same way Funaki did.

"You okay, Boudreaux?" Johnny asked, kneeling beside him. "It's just a spectator. Funaki wouldn't dare show his face around here."

"I thought I was over all that, Johnny," Boudreaux said.

"Is he all right?" asked one of the other golfers, concern showing in his face.

"It's nothing. He's just got a case of the jitters. This is his first big tournament. He'll be all right. Just give him a second to catch his breath."

After his heart rate and breathing returned to normal, Boudreaux slowly walked over to the trembling man.

"I'm sorry," the man said. "I did not mean to disturb you. I play here many times. De big pom tree tricks everybody new here. Sometimes, ball disappear in top branches."

"Thanks for the warning, sir." Boudreaux said as he reached out to shake the man's hand, feeling bad about his overreaction to the man's accent. "I don't mean to be rude, but are you from Japan?"

"Long time ago," the man said, cautiously. "My family come here in 1938, before war. When Japanese Navy attack Pearl Harbor, your government take my business and home and put my family and me in internment camp until war over. Terrible, terrible time. We lose everything. Have to start over. We were American citizens, same as you. Big shame."

"I heard about those things. I'm sorry. I guess there were some bad people on both sides in that war."

"Hey, Boudreaux. You gonna play or not?" one of his playing partners asked, giving a not-so-friendly look to the Japanese man.

"Yeah. Sorry about that," Boudreaux said over his shoulder. He shook the man's hand again, wished him and his family well, and returned to his ball, exhaling a sigh of relief. Having played this hole many times, he shared the man's awareness about how deceptive this hole, with the towering palm tree, could be to the uninitiated. He calmly and wisely punched a perfect, low grounder under the palm's expansive branches, leaving the ball two feet from the hole. He drained his short birdie putt.

The other three golfers, throwing caution (and the tournament) to the wind, elected to go over the palm tree. All three failed. In fact, all three balls got stuck in the uppermost branches, leaving the three golfers with double bogies.

As he walked to the fifth tee box, Boudreaux thought of the small, friendly Japanese man he had just met. *I've felt nothing but hatred for the Japanese people for five years,* he thought, as he headed for the green. *Maybe it's time I recognized the sad fact that we were all victims of this terrible war.*

Nobody laughed when Boudreaux did, indeed, take home the trophy and the prize money. Mickey was allowed the rare privilege of staying up late to help Boudreaux, Johnny, Augie, and Jane celebrate Boudreaux's victory. They were seated around one of the tables in the Whispering Hollows Grill.

"Boudreaux, I've got to hand it to you," Augie said, raising his beer in a toast. "I'm ashamed to admit I didn't think you could do it. You did in three months what no one, not even Robert Urquhart, could do in over forty years. You tamed the beast."

"Thanks, Augie, but I couldn't have done it without the help from everybody at this table. You, for giving me that wonderful, beautiful club. Johnny, for spending hours on the range and golf course helping me analyze and fine-tune my swing. Jane, for bringing Johnny and me lunch and dinner while we practiced for hours on end. Mickey...uh...well...for not farting during my backswing while I practiced."

"Hey!" Mickey yelled. "What about all these lumps and scars I got on my head from trying to dodge all those golf balls all over the pasture?"

Boudreaux laughed. "Just kidding, Mickey. I guess I should thank you most of all. Even though it's your own fault for not learning to duck a little faster, I do appreciate your shagging all those balls and diving into the bushes to retrieve the ones I sliced and hooked. You saved me a lot of money. Those balls aren't cheap."

Boudreaux leaned over and tousled Mickey's hair. "Besides, seeing you out there having fun reminded me of when I was your age, shagging balls for my old man. Mickey, above all, you remind me of what's really important in this world. Cheers, everybody! To a new beginning!"

The sounds of laughter and, once again, the clinking of beer bottles (and one root beer bottle) echoed out into the night air.

Chapter Eleven

Boudreaux kept a wary eye on the man partially hidden in the shadows of the aging pecan trees. The visitor sat quietly on the wooden bench, his inquisitive gaze hidden under the gray snap-brim cap. Boudreaux wasn't fooled. The man was observing him, studying his every move.

Boudreaux tried to ignore him as he teed up another ball, but he couldn't resist another glance at the stranger. He had spent the last three hours practicing shots with the Urquhart adjustable club and was pleased with his progress.

The man on the bench had mysteriously appeared within the last hour, and, except for his curious eyes, had remained motionless. A wooden cane leaned against the bench by his side. His handsome, angular face with its hawkish nose was marred by what appeared to be a couple of recently-healed scars over the left eye. His left arm was cradled in a loose sling. Boudreaux caught a glimpse of what looked like cloth bandages pressing out from between his slacks and high-ly-polished loafers.

He looks pretty banged up, Boudreaux thought. *Must have been in some sort of an accident.*

A few minutes later, another man joined his silent guest on the bench. They both appeared to be in their mid-thir-ties, but the second man towered over his companion. His friendly, hound dog eyes were in stark contrast to the dark, calculating eyes of the other man. They were both deeply tanned and had the rough, weather-beaten faces of men who spent a lot of time outdoors. The smaller man leaned over and whispered something to the other man, after which they both continued observing Boudreaux's workout.

Probably serious golfers, dropping by to gawk at the strange new kid with the funny-looking club. Boudreaux smiled to himself. *That's okay. I'll give them something to tell their friends about.*

Boudreaux continued practicing, trying, unsuccessfully, to put this curious twosome out of his mind. They didn't say much except for an occasional muted comment to each other. From the way they kept fiddling with their hands, as if mimicking his grip technique, Boudreaux realized they were more interested in studying his grip than the club he was using.

Boudreaux couldn't shake the feeling that he had seen these men somewhere before. It wasn't here at Whispering Hollows. Had they crossed paths during the war? Perhaps on the Bataan Death March or in one of the POW camps? Unable to place their faces, Boudreaux's curiosity got the better of him. He slowly sauntered over to the bench.

"Excuse me, but I couldn't help notice you were watching me practice. You two gentlemen look vaguely familiar. I'm Boudreaux James. Have we met?"

"I don't think so, son," the smaller man said. "But we've heard a lot about you and that revolutionary club you're using. From what we hear, you've been tearing up the competition with it. Good thing you didn't discover it earlier and use it in last year's U.S. Open. I'm afraid that trophy might be sitting in your trophy case instead of mine."

Boudreaux gasped, dropping his club to the ground. "Holy smokes!" he said, his eyes lighting up like beacons. "You're Ben Hogan."

The man laughed. "He's on to us, Byron," he said, looking at his smiling friend. "'Why don't you and Valerie come on down to our favorite getaway in the Hill Country for a couple of weeks?' you said. 'Nobody will recognize us.'"

Boudreaux slowly turned toward the other man, his face beaming in astonishment. "Byron Nelson? No wonder you two looked familiar." Boudreaux practically tripped over his feet as he enthusiastically leaned over to shake their hands. "You're the biggest names in golf. You were my idols when I was a kid."

The two living legends gave each other amused glances. "I don't think Sammy Snead would agree with that assessment," Byron Nelson said with a wink, "but we appreciate the compliment."

"I heard about your bad car accident in February, Mr. Hogan," Boudreaux said. "The newspapers said it might put a halt to your career."

"Don't count me out just yet, son. I broke some bones and had a few surgeries to fix some things, but the golf world hasn't heard the last of me. I may just surprise those folks who have already written me off."

Byron smiled, but his voice took on a somber tone. "Ben, I know you'll make it back, but for the time being you just need to think more about recuperating than jumping back out on the course too soon."

"All I'm saying, Byron, is I feel my best is still ahead of me."

"Actually," Byron said, glancing over Ben's shoulder, "your best is standing right behind you."

Their wives, Valerie Hogan and Louise Nelson, had quietly strolled up behind them. They both leaned over and kissed their husbands on the cheek.

"Ready for lunch, you two?" Louise asked.

"Give us a few minutes, would you?" Byron asked. "This young fella is Boudreaux James, the golfer we were telling you about the other day. He's the one who's hoping to some-day bring professional golf to its knees with his miraculous uni-club."

Everyone had a good laugh at the obvious absurdity of Byron's last statement. Deep down inside, however, Boudreaux wasn't laughing at all, for that's precisely what he and Johnny planned to do soon.

Ben and Byron introduced their wives to Boudreaux. The immense charm and graciousness of these attractive, genteel ladies left a great impression on him. After some small talk and promises to get together later, they all said their good-byes and parted company.

An hour later, Boudreaux and Johnny were in Augie's shop behind his office, tinkering with the Urquhart adjustable club. They had dismantled and oiled it and were carefully reassembling it.

Augie walked in and sat beside Boudreaux. "I heard you met our esteemed guests this afternoon. They were very impressed with you and your swing."

"I was shocked to see them here, Augie. Do they come here often?"

"Byron and his wife are regular guests. He retired from the tour several years ago to escape the pressure and bought a small cattle ranch near Fort Worth. They drive down here once or twice a year to get away from it all and relax. To protect their privacy, I don't mention it to anyone."

"Does Ben Hogan come here often, too?"

"No. This is his first time. I guess you heard about his car accident earlier this year."

"I read that he almost died in a head-on collision with a Greyhound bus somewhere in west Texas."

"He did nearly die that day. He would have if he hadn't leaned over to protect his wife before the impact. As he was attempting to cushion the blow to her body, the steering wheel snapped off and the steering column impaled his seat, right where his chest would have been." Augie paused and ran a trembling hand through his thinning hair.

He was wondering, sadly, if there had been something he could have done differently to save his wife's life in their own accident years ago. He dismissed the thought. "She escaped with some minor cuts and bruises, but he suffered deep cuts to his face, multiple broken bones, and some internal injuries," he continued.

"I remember reading a headline in *Time Magazine* calling him a hero," Boudreaux said. "Now I know why. He saved her life."

"That's right. Before the accident, he was a very private man. He was described by some as a cold fish, very blunt and unapproachable. His focus on playing was so intense he seldom acknowledged his fellow players, much less the fans."

"He seemed pretty friendly to me," Boudreaux said. "He and Byron seemed to be close buddies, too."

"As teenagers, they were friends. They even caddied together at Glen Garden Country Club in Fort Worth.

During their amateur and early pro years, their friendship continued, and they and their wives socialized quite a bit. Ben continued to get along well with the fans and fellow golfers for several years until the pressures of the tour and his competitive nature changed all that."

"What happened?" Boudreaux asked.

"In the 1930s, a great rivalry erupted between Ben, Byron, and another great player named Sam Snead. The competition between these men, who were considered the three greatest golfers of their day, escalated to the point where they barely spoke to one another. Byron, always the gentleman, retained his laid-back and amiable personality, but Ben and Sam let their bitterness interfere with their friendship. Ben's stoic and sometimes arrogant personality alienated many people, on and off the course. That's when his popularity waned."

"But then he changed?" Boudreaux said, beginning to understand.

"Yes, he changed. Tragedy does that to a person. It changed me, and I'm sure it changed you and Johnny."

"So, it was the accident," Boudreaux said.

"No. It was what happened after the accident that changed Ben. He knew he wasn't a popular man. Even Byron and Louise had stopped socializing with Ben and Valerie as much. Valerie stuck by him, though. She understood him. She understood his incessant desire to succeed, to be the best golfer in the world."

"What happened after the accident?" asked Johnny, who had been listening in rapt fascination to this discussion of a man he had heard of but had yet to meet.

"He received hundreds of phone calls, letters, and postcards from well-wishers. People he had never met were contacting him, offering their best regards, their prayers, and their hopes for a speedy recovery. Ben was overwhelmed to find there were so many people who cared about his welfare. He knew he didn't deserve this response, considering the way he had treated those around him. He was deeply touched. It's been said by some that he vowed to personally answer every single letter and postcard himself. That unexpected support might have been a key element in his desire to get well and return to the tour."

"Do you think he actually responded to every letter and postcard?" Boudreaux asked.

"I just met the man last week for the first time. I consider myself to be a pretty good judge of character, and by the look of determination in his eyes and the sincerity of his handshake, I don't doubt he responded to every single one. From what I heard, his icy demeanor melted quite a bit, and he now appreciates people more than he used to."

"I wish I'd been there with you, Boudreaux," Johnny said. "I would have really liked to meet those two. I'm about the same age as they are, and I've followed the stories about them ever since they were hotshot amateurs."

"Johnny, you'll be getting your wish," Augie said, with a satisfied look on his face. "They invited us, along with Jane and Mickey, to join them for a little get-together tonight."

Boudreaux and Johnny looked at each other and broke into broad grins.

"Hot diggity dog!" Johnny jumped up and pumped an excited fist into the air.

Byron and Ben had adjoining guest cabins that shared a large fire pit in back. The two men and their wives were relaxing in lawn chairs facing the fire pit, sipping ice-cold lemonade and staring quietly at the glowing coals. The burning embers rising from the flaming mesquite logs danced through the balmy night air like dazed lightning bugs.

Just after sundown, Augie, Jane, Mickey, Boudreaux, and Johnny appeared from around the corner of one of the cabins and approached the fire. Augie introduced Jane, Mickey, and Johnny to the two men and their wives. Louise and Valerie showed their graciousness by offering and serving lemonade to the late arrivals.

"Sorry we're late," Augie said. "We had to take care of a few things in the clubhouse."

"That's all right," Byron said. "We've just been sitting back enjoying this beautiful Texas sunset." The sky was orange where the sun had dipped below the horizon, and the first sprinkling of stars twinkled in the eastern sky.

Jane knew these living legends by reputation and wasn't about to miss out on the opportunity to meet them. She also felt it was very important for her son to meet them. *Wouldn't that be something for little Mickey to tell his kids and grandkids about someday?*

Byron looked at Boudreaux and then at Johnny. "Augie told me you two fought in the Pacific and had a pretty rough go of it over there in a few of those horrible POW camps."

"It wasn't exactly a Sunday school picnic," Johnny responded. "We were among the lucky ones to get out alive. A lot of the men we knew didn't make it back."

"You must have had a tremendous will to live," Ben said. "My hat's off to you."

Boudreaux added another log to the fire. "One of the things that kept me going," he said softly, "was thinking back on the days I spent caddying for my dad and then, when I was old enough, playing alongside him. I spent many days and nights reliving every round we had together. I never had the chance to tell him that. He died while I was gone."

"Your dad must have been pretty special," Ben said.

"Yes. He was my best friend."

Ben briefly looked over at his friend. "You know, Byron, I think the days you and I caddied together at Glen Garden were some of the happiest days of my life."

"I feel the same way," Byron said. "We didn't make much money, but we managed to have some fun."

"Did you two get started caddying for your dads?" Boudreaux asked.

"Neither of our dads golfed," Ben said. "We did it because our families needed the money. Especially mine, since my dad wasn't around." He lowered his head for a few seconds. "Would y'all excuse me for a minute?" he asked. He turned and walked a few paces away from the group. He put his hands in his pockets and stared at the star-studded horizon.

Byron leaned over to Boudreaux while glancing over his shoulder in Ben's direction. "Ben's father is a touchy subject, Boudreaux," he whispered. "I'd appreciate it if you didn't ask him anything else about his father."

"I'm sorry. What happened with his dad?"

"He committed suicide when Ben was a boy. Ben was in the next room and was the first to discover the body. It devastated him."

Ben's wife dabbed at a few tears forming in her eyes. "That was a long time ago," she said. "I thought he might be over it by now. You know, he didn't even tell me about it until long after we were married."

"That may be one of the reasons Ben has always been such a private, introverted person," Byron said. "I don't think that's something you ever get over."

After a few moments, Ben returned to his chair in front of the fire, his spirits apparently lifted by his brief time spent alone. "Sorry. A sudden breeze blew some smoke in my eyes." Ben fixed an affectionate eye on Mickey. "You haven't had much to say tonight, son. What are you thinking about?"

Mickey looked pleased to be included in the grown-up talk for a change. He beamed at the man everybody seemed to treat like royalty. "What I'm thinking about right now is how nice it would be to have a big, juicy hot dog and a long stick."

His mother playfully shoved his shoulder, as everyone around the fire pit had a good laugh. Byron laughed the hardest. "Usually, when people sit around a big camp fire," he said, "they get all thoughtful and ponder the meaning of the universe. But that boy's got the right idea. It takes a kid to really put things in perspective."

Mickey grinned sheepishly, but he had a triumphant look on his face.

"I like you, Mickey," Byron continued. "I wish I had a son just like you."

"Do you have any children, Mr. Nelson?" Jane asked.

"No. Louise and I would love to have a couple of kids, but it just hasn't been in the cards for us." He leaned over and patted his wife's knee and kissed her cheek. "Maybe, someday." Louise Nelson gave him a tender smile.

They had both accepted the fact that, for medical reasons, the only way they would ever be parents was through adoption. The only problem was that, even though Louise was in favor of adopting a child, her husband was hesitant to cross that bridge. *Maybe someday he'll change his mind,* she thought wistfully.

"You can borrow Mickey any time you like." Jane said with a laugh. "Dad told me you have a nice big ranch. I'm sure Mickey would be a big help around there."

"Wow! Can I?" Mickey blurted.

"That's up to Mr. and Mrs. Nelson, Mickey," Jane said.

Byron laughed, then leaned over and tousled the boy's hair. "You bet. That sounds like a great idea. Maybe you could come and visit us in late summer, before school starts. We've got a horse just about your size. He could use a new friend."

Mickey sat there, dreamily, for the rest of the evening with a big, lazy grin spread across his freckled face.

"Mr. Hogan, do you have any children?" Jane asked.

"Not yet," Ben replied. "We thought about it, but we both agreed that, with all the traveling going from tournament to tournament, a golfing life would be too hard on children. When I retire, we'll think about starting a family."

Valerie stole a brief glance at Louise. She wanted children just as badly as her friend did but understood the sacrifices a touring pro's wife must make.

Boudreaux thought about his first meeting with Ben and Byron. "Ben, when you and Byron were watching me earlier this afternoon, you seemed to be studying my grip. Did it seem unusual to you?"

"I noticed that all your shots were either straight as an arrow or had a slight fade. That's unusual. I was surprised that you never hooked the ball. Not once. I consider myself a pretty good ball-striker, but I've always had a problem with hooking the ball. My short game compensates for that, somewhat, but I'm afraid that until I solve that problem, I'll never reach my full potential. What's your secret?"

Boudreaux looked over at Johnny and smiled. "My secret? Believe it or not, my secret is Akio Funaki."

"Akio who?" Ben asked, looking confused.

"In that last POW camp Johnny and I were in before the war ended, we both took terrible beatings from Captain Akio Funaki, the camp commander. Johnny's injuries were worse than mine." He looked at his friend, then back at Ben. "Thank God we had each other to lean on. My left wrist was shattered and never healed properly. I can grip a club with it, but I can't bend it properly."

To demonstrate his problem, he grabbed a long, thin mesquite log and walked over to where Ben was sitting. He gripped it the way one would a golf club.

"See how crooked my left wrist is? I have to place my thumb on the top of the club instead of the recommended way which, as you know, is a little to the right. At impact with the ball, my wrist doesn't turn over as it should. That stiffness costs me a lot of distance, but, for some reason, it also prevents me from hooking the ball. Before the war, I had a terrible hook, too. Thanks to that beast, Funaki, it's gone."

"I'll be darned," Ben said, taking the log from Boudreaux. He tried out this restricted grip, which looked odd since his left arm was still in a sling. "Something as simple as that. I can't believe it. Thanks for the tip, Boudreaux. I can't wait to heal up a bit so I can try out your grip."

"My pleasure, Ben. I'd advise practicing with a real club instead of that log, though."

As Ben tossed the log into the fire, he and Byron both got a good laugh out of Boudreaux's last comment.

"I heard you surprised a lot of people down at Brackenridge last fall, running away with the tournament using that crazy-looking club of yours," Byron said.

"It did attract a lot of attention," Boudreaux replied, laughing. "There were a lot of skeptics at first, but afterward, I met a lot of converts. There was a big crowd of people wanting to take a closer look at that club."

"You may not realize it, Boudreaux, but you may have revolutionized the game of golf," Ben added. "And put some equipment manufacturers out of business."

"I doubt it," Boudreaux said, returning to his seat on a squat pecan tree stump. "I'll stick with it for personal reasons, but I'm sure, for others, it will always be just a novelty."

"That Brackenridge is one of our favorite courses. Isn't it, Ben?" Byron asked with a mischievous grin on his face.

"Speak for yourself, Byron," Ben said with a trace of annoyance in his voice.

"You've played there?" Jane asked them both.

"Aw, here we go again," Ben said with mock displeasure, giving a dismissive wave at his friend.

Byron chuckled. "Yes, that was a great week." He rose and held his hands over the dying coals. "It was 1940 when the Texas Open was held there. Ben and I were tied at the end of the final round and had to return Monday morning for an eighteen-hole playoff. He's never forgiven me for edging him by one stroke that day. I don't think he spoke to me for two weeks after that round."

"You just got lucky, Byron. It wasn't even that big a tournament."

"It was big to me," Boudreaux said, jumping up. "That was the first Texas Open Dad took me to. Watching you two battle it out was one of the most exciting things I ever saw."

Byron stood and stretched his lanky, six-foot-one frame. He gave Boudreaux a sly wink. "I'm glad someone besides me enjoyed it," he said playfully, then returned to his chair.

Ben just glared at Byron and shook his head.

"By the way," Byron said. "I've decided to take a short break from retirement and play in the U.S. Open this June. I'm thinking this year's trophy and the one I got in '39 will make nice bookends."

"Don't count those chickens too soon, Byron. I've signed up for it too."

"Ben, you can barely walk this course now. I know you're determined to get back out there, and I don't doubt you, but two months isn't that far away. There will be other U.S. Opens."

"I know," Ben said. "It's a long shot, but I think if I throw my hat in the ring, it will be a little extra motivation for me to get better. If I'm not ready, I'm not ready. Like you said, there will be other Opens. But I've got to try."

Augie enjoyed watching the playful ribbing between these two golfing greats. He stood and faced Boudreaux. "Wouldn't it be great, Boudreaux, if you qualified to compete in this year's U.S. Open? It is open to amateurs, you know. There's no money in it for you, but that trophy would look great in our clubhouse."

"I don't know if I'm good enough to play in a major," Boudreaux said. "Around here, I can hold my own, but on a national stage, I don't know. Besides, I'm sure there's a big fee involved plus traveling expenses. I don't even know how the qualification process works."

"There are two regional qualification sites," Byron said. "The nearest one this year, fortunately, is in Corpus Christi at the Oso Rojo Country Club. I don't know what the fee is, but the top forty qualifiers get to play in the U.S. Open. This year, it's being held at Medinah Country Club just outside of Chicago."

Augie beamed with excitement at Boudreaux. "Boudreaux, if you can save some money for the entry fee and traveling expenses to Corpus Christi, I'm sure I can get a little financial help from some of the club members. They all like you and Johnny. Then, if you qualify, I'm positive we can raise enough money to send you and Johnny to Medinah. I know the whole town would be thrilled to see a native son take on the big boys."

"What do you think, Johnny?" Boudreaux asked. "Do you think I'm ready for the big time?"

"Jeez, Boudreaux," Johnny said, excitedly. "You've been ready for months. Let's do it."

As the fire slowly died down and darkness settled over the well-manicured lawn, the sleepy group stood and said their goodnights to one another. All except Ben and Byron went back to their respective cabins. The only sound breaking the silence was the hiss and crackle of the few remaining embers.

"What do you think, Ben?" Byron asked, as he leaned back in his chair and folded his arms. "Can they do it? Boudreaux with that one club and poor Johnny barely able to hobble around this course? Do you think the world is ready for them?"

"Look at me, Byron. I'm a mess right now. I hurt all over, and I'm still not sure if this old body will bounce back. I didn't want to say this in front of Valerie and Louise, but I was thinking of just quitting the game if I couldn't give it 100%. That is, until I met Boudreaux and Johnny. Look at those two. If anyone ever had a right to throw in the towel, it's them. But you could see it in their eyes. They went through hell and back and are thrilled just to be alive and have one more chance at life."

Ben bent over the ashes and gingerly picked up the half-burned log Boudreaux had used to show his golf grip. "Do I think they can do it? Absolutely. And, if they can beat the odds and plow ahead with that much optimism, then who's to say I can't? I've made up my mind, Byron. Like them, I refuse to give up. God spared me for a reason, too. Surviving that accident and meeting those two boys made me re-think a few things. I may not make it back this year to defend my title, but I will make it back. I still believe my best is still ahead of me."

As the ashes cooled, the yellow moon slowly dipped behind the majestic live oaks. The two men sat quietly and motionless, each pondering his fate and place in golf history.

As fate would have it, Byron played poorly in the 1949 U.S. Open and missed the cut. Immediately afterwards, he returned to the quiet life of a country squire tending his cattle and chickens, only venturing out for the occasional tournament to honor his many fans and the game he dearly loved.

Ben's broken body had not healed fast enough to allow him to honor his commitment to that year's U.S. Open. Nevertheless, he kept his word to never give up and continued his strict regimen of exercise and practice. He did make it to the 1950 U.S. Open—which he won. He also entered the 1951 U.S. Open and won that, too. Not surprisingly to those who knew him, he won it again in 1953. At that point, he had attained his goal of being recognized as the greatest golfer in the world.

Chapter Twelve

Business in the Whispering Hollows Grill was slow. The late afternoon rush was over, and Boudreaux and Johnny sat at a corner table brainstorming—trying to think up ways to come up with the fee for the U.S. Open qualification rounds next month in Corpus Christi.

Jane made it perfectly clear that Boudreaux and Johnny were not going without her. With all the moral support she and her son had invested in Boudreaux's quest, she felt they had earned the right to go with them. Besides, she had already promised Mickey that when school was out for the summer, she would take him to the coast. She tried to take him down there at least once a year during summer vacation.

He loved it when kids he met on the beach asked him what happened to his mother's arm. His morbid sense of humor emerged when he dramatically fabricated a tale of how a great white shark had bitten off her arm while she was pearl diving. He delighted in their awestruck, rapt attention as he explained how his mom used her right hand to gouge out the shark's eyes, resulting in its recoiling and dashing away in fear. That fib was enough to make him the most popular and respected kid on the beach. Jane was always a little perplexed at the sight of the reverential stares she received from the kids and the deference they showed her son. Mickey never told her the reason why. She just assumed they were curious about her deformity.

"Between the two of us," Boudreaux said with a frown, "we might scrape up enough to cover part of it. Augie said he would lend us his Studebaker, but we've still got to come up with enough money to buy gas and food."

"We could borrow some money from some of the club members," Johnny said. "I'm sure they would help us out."

"No. Augie said he would hit them up for the cost of the trip to Medinah if I qualify, but I don't want to go begging twice."

"I understand, Boudreaux. You've got your pride. Maybe you could hustle up a few more jobs giving golf lessons."

"I've tried, but money's tight, and that business doesn't start to pick up until summer vacation."

Boudreaux glanced up as a husky, weather-beaten, middle-aged man approached the counter.

"Evening, sir. What can I get you?" Jane asked, laying the bar towel she was holding over her partial left arm as was her habit. Even after all these years, she was still a little self-conscious of the inevitable stares of strangers.

"I'd like a Coca-Cola, miss," the man said, taking a slow look around the room, his gaze resting briefly on Boudreaux and Johnny. "And a ham and cheese on rye, if you've got it."

"You bet," Jane replied.

While the stranger settled comfortably onto one of the bar stools, his attention was drawn to a young boy fiddling with the knobs of an old Philco radio at the end of the counter. Mickey stopped playing with the radio long enough to give the man the once-over. His curiosity satisfied, he returned to the task of finding a suitable station on the radio.

Jane served the man his sandwich and drink, then returned to cleaning the counter top. Eventually, the squawking and loud static emitting from the radio, a result of Mickey's incessant knob-turning, got on the man's nerves.

"Excuse me, son," he said mildly. "Would you just pick a station? That noise is giving me a headache."

Mickey stopped and looked over at the man. *Who is this old fart cussing at me?* he thought. He smiled innocently for a few seconds, then stuck his index fingers in the corners of his mouth, stretched it open as wide as possible, stuck out his tongue, crossed one eye, and let loose with a loud "Pbbbt!" Pleased with his bold response to this interloper, Mickey resumed his channel searching.

"Knock it off, you little monster!" the exasperated man yelled as he stood and gave the startled boy a withering look.

A half-second later, a thin arm snaked across the counter catching the man by his beefy left wrist. He turned and looked at the petite, blonde waitress with the fiery look in her eyes, who maintained her grip on him like a vice.

"I apologize for my son's poor manners, mister. He may be a little monster, but he's *my* little monster. If you ever want to use this arm again, I'd advise you to not call him names again."

Jane gave Mickey a stern look and jerked her head toward the grill's entrance. Mickey obediently leapt off his bar stool and scampered out the front door in search of other adventures. The man pulled his arm out of Jane's grasp, picked up his drink and sandwich, and headed out the door to finish his lunch on the patio.

Boudreaux and Johnny had watched the confrontation with amusement, then looked at each other and laughed.

"Let's go outside, Johnny," Boudreaux said. "It ain't safe around here when Jane's on the warpath."

They gave Jane friendly waves, then took their bottles of beer outside to the patio. Settling into a couple of Adirondack chairs, they discreetly observed the chastised man sitting at a table a few yards away. Rubbing his left wrist, he glanced over at Boudreaux and Johnny.

"Did you see that?" he asked. "That crazy woman's got a grip like a bear."

Johnny grinned. "It's not wise to fool with mama bear."

"I guess not," the man said. "What that little ragamuffin needs is a good whipping."

Boudreaux decided he didn't like this man very much. "The kid's all right," he said. "He's just a little rambunctious, as most boys his age are. There was no need for you to call him a little monster, especially in front of his mother."

The man nodded, realizing he was a little hasty, then gave Boudreaux a hard look.

"Say, aren't you Boudreaux James? The kid who's making a name for himself taking on all comers with that funny adjustable club?"

"One and the same," Boudreaux replied with a laugh. He stood, walked over to the man and extended his hand. "I don't believe I've had the pleasure."

"My name's Alvin Thompson. I just drove down from Fort Worth for a little vacation. Thought I'd get in a few rounds of golf."

"Are you a rancher?" Boudreaux asked.

"No. I'm an entrepreneur, you might say. Just doing a little business in north Texas. I needed to take a break from the stench of those infernal stockyards."

Boudreaux and Johnny exchanged glances. *The old codger doesn't know the meaning of the word stench,* Boudreaux thought. *Now I know I don't like him.*

Boudreaux decided he'd had enough of this man. He excused himself and returned to his chair to continue his brainstorming with Johnny, but the man had other ideas.

"Mind if I join you boys?" Alvin asked, as he ambled over to their table.

"No, have a seat, Mr. Thompson," Boudreaux said, reluctantly, not wanting to be rude. "This is my friend, Johnny Frye."

"Pleasure to meet you. Please, call me Alvin. Tell me, Boudreaux, how good are you with this club of yours? Are you just beating the local duffers, or are you good enough to take on serious players?"

"I've proved I can hold my own against some pretty decent golfers. How's your game?"

"I don't like to brag, son, but I think I still might be good enough to teach you young pups a thing or two."

What an arrogant jerk, Boudreaux thought. He was liking this man less and less.

"Are you a betting man, Boudreaux?"

Boudreaux wasn't sure he liked where this conversation was going. *Is this man just looking for a little money game, or is he one of those out-of-town hustlers looking for an easy mark?*

"Why do you ask, Alvin?"

"I'll admit I'm not quite the young buck I used to be, but I don't think there's anyone in the world who could beat me in a round of golf with just one club. Doesn't seem natural, somehow."

"I'll bet Boudreaux could whip you on his worst day," Johnny said defensively. He didn't seem too fond of this blowhard, either.

Boudreaux glared at his loyal, but impetuous, friend. "Stay out of this, Johnny."

"Come on, Boudreaux," Johnny continued. "This fella's just yanking your chain. We both know you can beat him."

With an amused look, Alvin Thompson looked at Johnny, then at Boudreaux, who said nothing.

"Well, Boudreaux, it looks like your friend has more confidence in your game than you do. That's a shame. If you don't feel you're up to the challenge, I understand. Here, you'll always be a big fish in a small pond. Go ahead and stay here and enjoy playing the big shot to the locals. By all means, don't try to bite off more than you can chew."

Concluding his little speech, Alvin Thompson rose and left the table, chuckling under his breath, knowing the hook was set.

"You're on," Boudreaux said, before Alvin had returned to his table.

"What's that, son?" Alvin asked, slowly turning with an innocent look on his face.

"I said, you're on."

"All right. How about this Wednesday morning at 8:00? For, let's say, one hundred dollars. Can you handle that?"

"One hundred dollars is just fine," Boudreaux said. "No checks, cash only. Understood?" Boudreaux still didn't trust this man any more than he could throw him.

"Sure," Alvin said. "I'll see you Wednesday morning." He paused for a minute, scratching his chin. "I'll tell you what, Boudreaux. Since I like you, I'll give you a sporting chance.

I'll play the front nine holes right-handed and the back nine holes left-handed, providing you agree to up the stakes to two hundred dollars. Sound fair?"

"That's fine by me," Boudreaux said as he looked over at an astonished Johnny. *I'm beginning to think this guy is nuts. This could be the easiest money I ever earned.*

As Alvin walked away, Boudreaux and Johnny stared at each other in disbelief. They were both wondering whether this was a stroke of good fortune or if they had inadvertently stumbled into something that was way over their heads. They would find out Wednesday.

Chapter Thirteen

"**A**re you two out of your cotton-pickin' minds?" Augie asked as he looked incredulously at Boudreaux and Johnny, seated on the other side of the grill's corner table. They both wore the embarrassed look of schoolboys who might have just been caught smoking in the boys' lavatory.

"I can't believe you bet a total stranger two hundred dollars on one round of golf."

Seated on each side of Augie were Ben Hogan and Byron Nelson. The three of them had been enjoying a late afternoon drink (bourbon for Augie and Ben and lemonade for the teetotaler Byron) while reminiscing about the old days on the professional golf circuit.

"The man's got to be in his fifties," Johnny said defensively. "There's no way he can beat Boudreaux."

"Do you know anything at all about this Alvin Thompson?" Augie asked.

"He's a businessman from north Texas, down here on vacation." Boudreaux said. "How good could that old man be?"

"He was even dumb enough to offer to play the front nine right-handed and the back nine left-handed," Johnny added.

Augie rolled his eyes in exasperation. "For your information, smart guys, I do know something about this Alvin Thompson. He's more commonly known as "Titanic" Thompson, and he's a professional hustler from way back before you two were even born. One of his earliest victims gave him that nickname, because he sinks everybody he bets."

Boudreaux and Johnny looked at each other with the slack-jawed comprehension that they may have been taken for a ride.

"Titanic doesn't take vacations," Ben said, finally joining the conversation. "This is just another business trip for him."

"That's right," said Byron. "He bounces from country club to country club looking for wealthy members to fleece. He's also ambidextrous. One of his favorite cons is to beat his opponent right-handed, then offer to play another round, double or nothing, left-handed. Since he's a natural lefty, he always wins. It looks like your goose is cooked, Boudreaux."

"How do the three of you know all this?"

Augie, Ben, and Byron gave each other knowing looks.

Ben spoke first. "Boudreaux, in the 1930s, Titanic Thompson was known far and wide as a traveling hustler who was an expert at billiards, sharpshooting, cards, craps, golf, you name it. And the man had a knack for coercing people into betting on just about anything."

"He apparently had excellent hand-eye coordination," Byron said. "He also studied gambling odds. He made a lot of money in his day. I heard the only time he ever lost money was on horse races."

"Believe it or not, Boudreaux," Ben said, "Augie, Byron, and I have played against him at one time or another. Titanic and I were never what you would call friends, but we did partner up several times in a few small money matches. That's not something I'm proud of, since he wasn't above cheating if he could get away with it, but money was tight in those days. I wish I'd known he was down here working. I would have advised you to steer clear of him."

"Ben's right," Bryon said. "He probably picked you out when he realized no other suckers were available at the moment. No offense intended."

"None taken," Boudreaux said. "I asked for it."

Augie rose from his chair, walked around the table, and placed a hand on Boudreaux's shoulder. "He played you, Boudreaux," Augie said. "You're good, but that old man, as you called him, has probably got enough game left in him to run circles around you. He said the only reason he never turned pro was he didn't want to take a cut in pay."

"I think I'm in trouble, Johnny," Boudreaux said. "Maybe I can get Alvin—I mean, Titanic—to cancel our bet. I'll tell him I'm coming down with something."

"I wouldn't count on it, boys," Augie said. "When Titanic smells blood, he goes in for the kill. He's not the type to let a little fish like you off the hook. I doubt he even needs the money. He likes to scam hotshots like you just for the thrill of it. Do you even have two hundred dollars, Boudreaux?"

"No," Boudreaux said, obviously dejected. "Right now, I'd be lucky to scrape up twenty dollars."

"Well, you'd better figure out a way to scrape it up pretty fast and be prepared for the worst," Augie said. "I'll try to help you out, but if you lose, your chance of making it to the qualification rounds down in Corpus Christi will be pretty slim."

"Boudreaux's a big tough guy," Johnny said hopefully. "Maybe he could let Titanic know he found out about his past reputation as a hustler and persuade him that it would be in his best interest to call off the bet."

Augie smiled. "Did I mention he's killed five people? All over little *misunderstandings* over money?"

"Okay," a startled Johnny said, quickly downing a large swig of his beer. "What do you say we just forget that stupid idea?"

After a few moments of silence, Johnny perked up, snapping his fingers. "Wait a second. I think I have a better idea."

Augie pressed the palms of his hands against his forehead. "Oh, Lord, help us. Johnny's got another idea. The man who got Boudreaux in this fix in the first place has a plan."

"No, seriously," Johnny said, rising from his chair and rubbing his chin pensively. "This could work. You say he's a con man, right? Well, who says you can't con a con man? We'll beat him at his own game."

"What are you talking about, Johnny?" Boudreaux asked.

"I've always had a little con man in me. If you remember, Boudreaux, I got us out of a few tight spots back in those days in the Pacific."

"You're right, Johnny, but that was a long time ago. Things have changed a lot since then."

"Not for me, Boudreaux. Not for me. I don't like bullies of any stripe, and right now I'd like nothing better than the chance to turn the tables on that pompous jerk."

"Okay. I'm listening, Johnny," Boudreaux said.

"Yeah," Byron said gleefully. "I can't wait to hear this."

Ben looked in amazement at the animated faces around the table. "I hope you boys aren't planning on doing anything illegal. If you are, keep me and Byron out of it. We've got reputations to uphold." After saying his piece, he grinned and rubbed his hands together. "I do hope it's good, though. That man still owes me my half of the fifty dollars in winnings from our last *partnership* match. He conveniently forgot to give me my share before he left town."

"First, it will take some cooperation from you, Boudreaux," Johnny said. "And Jane, too, assuming she's got a wicked sense of humor and a strong stomach. There's no guarantee it will work, but it's worth a try."

"What's your great plan, Johnny?" Boudreaux asked. "Do we break his arm? Kidnap him? Kill him and bury his dismembered body parts under the eighteenth green?"

Augie's eyes grew wide. Apparently, he failed to see the humor in this line of talk. "Hold it, boys. It's just a two-hundred-dollar bet. No need to resort to violence. You two have already spent enough time locked up."

"No, nothing like that," Johnny said. "My plan is based on an old trick my dad and I used a couple of times in Missouri to win turkey shoot competitions."

"What did you do?" Boudreaux asked.

"Dad was on friendly terms with a couple of the downtown hookers. He persuaded them (with a little cash contribution) to hide in the woods next to the shooting range. Right before the first competitor raised his rifle to take a shot, they would burst from the trees, run directly in front of him, stark naked, screaming and hollering, and then disappear into the trees on the other side of the range. The spectators loved it, but the other shooters didn't have time to regain enough composure to get off a decent shot. Cool as cucumbers, Dad and I calmly stepped up and managed to take first prize both times."

Johnny called Jane out from the grill's kitchen and asked her to join them at the table. For the next hour, Johnny explained in detail to the entire group his plan to win the two-hundred-dollar bet with Titanic Thompson.

If this works, Johnny thought, *folks around these parts will be talking about this little escapade for years.*

When Johnny was done explaining the plan, the rest of the group looked at each other for a quiet moment. Then, as if on cue, they all burst out laughing and agreed it could work.

Afterwards, in the parking lot, Byron and Ben stood by themselves and made an agreement that if the plan didn't work out, they would anonymously slip an envelope with three hundred dollars under Boudreaux's cabin door. Two hundred would pay off the bet with Titanic, and the extra hundred should be enough to cover Boudreaux's entry fee and expenses for the qualifying rounds. They both had grown immensely fond of Boudreaux and Johnny and wanted them to succeed.

Chapter Fourteen

That evening, after closing time, Boudreaux, Johnny, and Jane sat together at one of the grill's tables, going over the list of items they needed for their plan. They all agreed this bizarre idea of Johnny's would be a beauty—if it worked.

"Most of this stuff we can get at the hardware store and right here in the grill," Johnny explained.

Boudreaux pointed a finger at the bottom of the list. "Jane, you'll need to talk to Dottie at her dress shop on Main Street about this last item. It's the most important part of our plan."

"What do I tell her?" Jane asked.

"Don't tell her the real reason you need it. Just make something up. If she turns you down, *borrow* it when she's not looking. You can sneak it back in later."

"Got it," Jane said. "If it's okay with you boys, I'd like to bring Mickey in on this. After the way that man talked to him in the grill, I know he'd like to get him back."

Boudreaux looked at Johnny, who nodded his approval.

"Okay," Boudreaux said. "That might make it a little more interesting. If anybody asks any questions about what we're up to, don't say anything. If this backfires, I don't want it getting back to the club members. We could all lose our jobs."

"Yeah, we got it, Boudreaux," Johnny said. "What's our signal going to be?"

Boudreaux pushed the list aside then cupped his hands in front of him. "I'm getting to that. After we finish the front nine, if I'm beating the socks off of him, say, by nine strokes or more, you do nothing. He won't be able to catch me by then."

Boudreaux tried to ignore the disbelieving smirk on Johnny's face. "Okay, Johnny, I know that's a little optimistic. Just stay hidden and follow along just in case, by some miracle, he catches up to me."

"Then what?" Johnny asked.

"If I feel he's getting a little too close for comfort, look for me to take my hat off and scratch my head. That's when I'll excuse myself, saying I've got to see a man about a horse. When I'm behind the nearest tree, taking care of business, that's when you spring into action. When you're done, and, hopefully, this won't take more than five minutes, I'll come back out acting as if I have no clue as to what happened. You all need to be gone by then. I hope to God this works, or I'm going to look like a fool."

"Or a corpse," Johnny said, half seriously. "Don't worry, Boudreaux. If it doesn't work out as planned, Titanic may just end up fertilizing some of those new crape myrtles I just planted alongside the eighteenth fairway."

Boudreaux gave Johnny a shocked look. I *don't know if Johnny's kidding or not. I'd better keep a sharp eye on him.*

At a quarter to eight Wednesday morning, Boudreaux and Titanic stood next to each other on the tee box waiting for Augie to arrive. The air was crisp, and a slight sheen of dew covered the fresh-mown grass of the first fairway.

Glimmering rays of sunshine reflected off the rolling hills, giving the course an otherworldly aura.

Boudreaux never grew tired of the magnificent view of the undulating green in the distance. This was his front-row pew in church. It was where he took pause every morning to give thanks to God for sparing his and Johnny's lives and to reflect on how he would make the most of his remaining years.

His first priority was to take care of Johnny. He had recently noticed subtle changes in Johnny's ability to remember even the most basic things. His limp had grown more noticeable as well. Boudreaux and Johnny had been warned by the Army doctors that this might happen sooner or later. Boudreaux's wounds were mostly psychological and would heal with time, but Johnny's were acutely physical as well as psychological. Johnny knew this and had accepted it. He knew his friend would look after him and never desert him.

"Ready to see who has the honors, Boudreaux?" Augie asked, snapping Boudreaux out of his reverie. He had arrived promptly at eight to witness the start of the match.

"Sure," Boudreaux replied. He pulled a tee from his pocket and handed it to Augie, who tossed it up in the air in a circular motion. The tee hit the ground between the two competitors. It pointed to Alvin.

"I'm up," Alvin said, as he courteously bent over to pick up the tee. He held it briefly in the palm of his hand inspecting it with a curious look on his face. The tee was slightly scuffed and was cracked in the middle, leaving the cupped end at a slight angle.

"You always save your broken tees, Boudreaux?" he asked.

"Unfortunately, those are the only kind I have. I don't get paid that much. I can't afford new tees like the members here."

Alvin looked over at Augie who raised his hands in defense.

"Hey," Augie said. "I don't set the employees' salaries. That's up to management."

Alvin dug into his bag and brought out a handful of tees. "Here, Boudreaux, take some of mine. I've got plenty."

"Thanks, Alvin, but no. I've managed to get by this long with these used tees. I'm not going to change now. Besides," Boudreaux said with a laugh, "I don't think this poor old club of mine would know what to do if it saw a new tee."

"Suit yourself," Alvin said, shaking his head. He stood looking at Boudreaux for a long moment, then walked over to him, leaned in close so Augie wouldn't hear him and looked him dead in the eye.

"Boudreaux, to tell you the truth, I do this for a living, and I can't say I'm always proud of the way I conduct business. I don't mind taking a few bucks off wealthy country club golfers, but..." His voice trailed off for a few seconds. "You don't even have two hundred dollars, do you?"

"Don't worry about me, Alvin. If you beat me, I promise you I'm good for the money."

"I admire your spunk and your sense of honor, Boudreaux, but we can call it quits right now if you want. There will be no hard feelings, and we can part friends."

"Thanks, Alvin, but I have confidence in my game, and a bet is a bet. I believe you're up."

"I've got some work to do," Augie said, as he turned to leave. "I'll see you two after the round."

Augie would have liked nothing better than to follow along to observe Johnny's plan, but didn't want to be in the vicinity in case something went wrong. What was about to take place was strictly between Alvin, Boudreaux, Johnny, Jane, and Mickey.

Alvin nodded to Augie and teed up his ball. After addressing the ball and lining up his shot, he split the fairway with a low, crushing drive.

After teeing up his ball, Boudreaux double-checked the setting on his adjustable club then nailed a perfect drive twenty yards short of Alvin's.

Before they left the tee box, Alvin asked Boudreaux if he would show him how his club worked. "Craziest thing I've ever seen," Alvin said in awe. "I may just try to find myself one of these gadgets. There's got to be some sort of angle I can figure out to make some money off this."

Boudreaux didn't hit his drives nearly as far as Alvin did, but his consistency kept the scoring close. They traded leads several times until the eighth hole, when a bad slice put Boudreaux's ball out of bounds. After double-bogeying the hole and bogeying the ninth, he made the turn three strokes behind Alvin. Things weren't looking good for Boudreaux.

Before heading to the tenth tee box, Alvin went to the clubhouse to exchange his right-handed clubs for a left-handed set, as per their agreement.

Upon returning, Alvin lightly touched Boudreaux on the shoulder. "Augie told me a little about the terrible ordeal you and Johnny endured during the war. You must have been awful tough fellows to survive that."

"It was three years of pure hell, but we learned a lot from it. We learned the value of friendship and to appreciate everything we have—even broken tees."

Alvin smiled and nodded his head in understanding. "You and Johnny would do anything for each other, wouldn't you?"

"You bet we would."

"I wish I had a friend like that," Alvin said. "I was drafted during the Great War, but I was one of the lucky ones who never had to face the enemy. I spent my time stateside training other draftees—and gambling. I made a lot of money but not many friends. I guess I could learn a few things from you and Johnny."

Alvin doesn't seem like such a bad guy, Boudreaux thought. *Maybe I misjudged him.*

"I'm three up, Boudreaux, and I feel it only fair to warn you I can play as well left-handed as I can right-handed. Are you sure you don't want to cancel the match?"

"No. A bet's a bet," Boudreaux said, with a slight twinge of guilt but feeling he was in too deep to back out now.

Alvin had the honors, and both men hit perfect drives down the middle of the tenth fairway. After reaching his ball, Boudreaux took a moment to survey his shot then hit a high, slight draw to the left center of the green. They walked side by side another fifteen yards to Alvin's ball. Boudreaux decided it was time to execute Johnny's plan. But first, he decided he needed to ask Alvin a question.

"Alvin, is it true you shot five men dead? Just over money?"

Surprised by the question, Alvin turned toward Boudreaux. "That's an absolute lie," Alvin declared with indignation.

His face softened a little. "Actually, I only shot four men dead. In each case, they were crooks trying to rob me of my gambling winnings. No loss to humanity as far as I was concerned. The fifth man I killed with a hammer. The fool tossed me off my own boat and threatened a lady friend of mine. I was vindicated on all accounts."

Maybe this wasn't such a good idea after all, Boudreaux thought.

"Alvin, give me a second before you hit, will you?" Boudreaux removed his hat and scratched his head. "I need to see a man about a horse."

"All right," Alvin replied. "Take your time."

Boudreaux walked toward a large live oak alongside the fairway then disappeared behind it. Five seconds later, a blood-curdling scream came from the other side of the fairway, fifty yards from where Alvin was lining up his second shot.

"What the—?" Alvin yelled, as a young woman bolted from a stand of trees. She ran across the fairway directly in front of him. She wore a blood-stained blouse hanging in tatters from her thin frame.

"Help! Help!" she screamed. "He's trying to kill me." Her right hand held her dangling, bloody left arm. Only it wasn't a full arm. The lower half below the elbow was missing, the raw stump dripping blood on the grass, leaving a zig-zag pattern of stains as she ran for her life. "He cut off my arm. Somebody help me, please!"

Following close behind her was a man with a hat pulled low over his face, wielding a bloody machete. "Come back here, you sorry tramp!" he screamed, menacingly. "I'll teach you to cheat on me. I'll cut your other arm off!"

Alvin looked on in shock at the bizarre sight unfolding before his eyes, but what happened next sent him over the edge. Trailing the deranged man was a young boy, waving what looked like a short stick at the man's back, occasionally connecting with a slapping sound. Alvin recoiled in horror when he realized it wasn't a stick the boy was holding. It was the woman's bloody, severed forearm, the boy gripping it by the wrist with both hands.

"Daddy, don't kill my mama!" the boy cried. "Don't kill my mama!"

Unable to control himself, Alvin doubled over and retched in the grass at his feet. His knees gave way, and he collapsed to the ground, seemingly unable to register what just happened. After wiping his mouth clean, he sat up and looked around. All that remained of the gruesome episode was a trail of blood from one side of the fairway to the other. As quickly as the three had appeared, they had disappeared into the trees, the screaming and hollering fading into the distance.

A minute later, a whistling Boudreaux casually strolled out from behind the big tree, having taken care of business. Seeing Alvin sitting on the ground with a shocked look on his face, Boudreaux quickly walked over to him.

"You okay, Alvin? You don't look so good."

"Did...did you just see that, Boudreaux?" Alvin stuttered. "Some maniac with a machete just chased a one-armed girl across the fairway. He must have just cut her arm off and was trying to finish her off. And then this screaming little kid was hot on the man's heels hitting him with the same arm he had just cut off. Don't tell me you didn't hear any of it."

"You been drinking, Alvin?" Boudreaux asked, with mock concern in his voice. "That's about the craziest story I've ever heard. I did hear some yelling, but I figured it was someone celebrating a hole-in-one or something."

Boudreaux helped Alvin to his feet, noticing a slight tremble in the man's hands. "After the round, you should lie down and get some rest. I think the heat is getting to you."

"I can't go on, Boudreaux. I'm heading back to the club-house." Alvin wiped his face with his golf towel. "Either I'm going crazy, or the people in this part of the country are nuts."

"What about our bet, Alvin?" Boudreaux said, with disguised satisfaction. "Remember, a bet is a bet."

Alvin reached in his golf bag for his wallet and pulled out two one-hundred-dollar bills and practically threw them at Boudreaux. "Here's your money. I've had it with this place. I'm heading back to Fort Worth tonight where people are more civilized."

Alvin grabbed his clubs and returned to the clubhouse, waving his arms and mumbling to himself.

I guess it is possible to con a con man, Boudreaux thought, as he carefully inspected the two crisp one-hundred-dollar bills in his hands, satisfied that they were genuine and not counterfeit. He still didn't have any reason to completely trust Alvin.

Chapter Fifteen

The next morning, Boudreaux, Johnny, Augie, Jane, and Mickey sat at their favorite table on the grill's patio enjoying a leisurely breakfast. They were discussing the clever scam they had pulled, marveling at how well it worked.

"I say good riddance to him," Johnny said. "He got what he deserved. I just hope he never catches on to what we did. No telling what that man would do."

What they had not counted on was Alvin delaying his departure until that morning and dropping by the grill to say farewell to Boudreaux and Johnny.

"Hi Boudreaux, Johnny," Alvin said. "I just wanted to stop by and say goodbye and wish you luck at the U.S. Open qualification down in Corpus Christi."

"Thanks, Alvin," Boudreaux said. "That two hundred bucks saved the day."

"That's great. You know, I've been thinking about that crazy club of yours. I have some creative ideas about how I can earn back that two hundred dollars that I lost to you, plus some, if I can get my hands on one of those."

As Alvin turned to leave, he froze in his tracks. He slowly glanced at the others at the table. Johnny was wearing a hat identical to the one the machete-wielding maniac was wearing. His gaze then turned to the young woman whose left arm terminated just below the elbow. Perfectly healed, no sign of trauma. He turned toward the little boy. The last time he saw him, he was swinging a severed arm. For the next ten seconds, the five seated at the table wore frozen expressions. No one spoke.

"What . . . ? Wait a minute." Alvin said, in an almost inaudible whisper. Gradually, a broad, understanding grin spread across his face. "All right, whose idea was it?"

After a few moments of uncomfortable silence, Johnny raised a hand. "Don't blame them. It was my idea."

"I hate to admit it, Johnny, but that was one of the best cons I've ever seen. I don't know where you got the fake arm, but the blood was a nice touch." He leaned over and picked up a fresh bottle of ketchup, eyeing it closely. "I don't have to guess where that came from."

"I hope there's no hard feelings," Boudreaux said, "I mean, Augie told us about your being an expert golfer right- or left-handed and how you weren't above bending the rules and the odds in your favor occasionally."

"Oh, he did, did he? I guess the way word gets around nowadays, I'd better be more careful who I bet with. No, Boudreaux, no hard feelings, though not too many people pull the wool over Titanic Thompson's eyes and live to tell about it."

Alvin paused a few seconds to let those last words sink in. "It's like they say, 'Fool me once, shame on you. Fool me twice, bang, you're dead.'" Alvin continued. "I've got something for you, Johnny," he said, as he slowly slipped his right hand underneath the left lapel of his sport coat.

Oh, no, he's reaching for a gun, Boudreaux thought. *Is Johnny going to be number six?*

Instead of a gun, Alvin brought out a business card and flicked it on the table next to Johnny's beer. "I like your style, Johnny. If you ever want to make some serious money, look me up. We'd make a great team."

"Thanks, Alvin. I appreciate the offer, but I've got all the team I need right here."

"I believe you're right, Johnny. Boudreaux, I expect to hear good things about you next month at Medinah."

Alvin walked over to Mickey and leaned in close. "As for you, you little whipper-snapper." Alvin then stuck his fingers in his mouth, stretched it wide open, and crossed one eye. "Pbbbt," he said to a surprised, and obviously delighted, Mickey.

"So long, Alvin," Boudreaux said. "And thanks."

After the rest of the group said their farewells, Alvin "Titanic" Thompson hopped into his convertible Cadillac and sped down the winding drive to the main road then disappeared in a cloud of dust.

"We sure pulled one over on him," Johnny said, triumphantly.

Augie let forth a burst of laughter that reverberated throughout the patio.

"It wasn't that funny, Augie," Boudreaux said in a contemplative mood. He thought back to the moment on the tenth tee when Alvin offered to let him off the hook.

"Oh, yes it was," Augie said. "He played you again. You didn't fool that man."

"What do you mean?" Johnny asked, leaning forward in his chair.

"Last night, he dropped by my cabin to tell me about your little escapade. He thought it was brilliant."

"You mean to tell me he knew it was staged?" Johnny asked. "What tipped him off?"

"When Boudreaux introduced you to him the other day on the patio, your last name rang a bell. Frye isn't a common name, but, apparently, it's one that's well known in southern Missouri. When I told him you were from the Ozarks, he put two and two together."

"I don't follow you," Johnny said.

"You mentioned you got the idea from the old turkey shoot competition scam you and your old man pulled in the Ozarks. Did I mention Titanic was born in the Ozark Mountains about fifty miles from where you were raised? His family moved to Arkansas when he was a boy, but long before then, his father and your father knew each other. They hunted and fished together. They were friends. Who do you think your dad learned that trick from? He learned it from Titanic's dad, who taught it to Titanic."

Understanding slowly began to register in Johnny's eyes. "I'll be tarred and feathered!" he said.

"The screaming caught him off guard at first, but it didn't take him long to realize what was going on. Especially when he remembered his first meeting with you, Jane. He's got a sharp eye. He said he caught a glimpse of your left arm before you covered it with the towel. That's not something you easily forget. He let the two of you get away with it partly because he liked and respected you, but mostly because he was impressed with your ingenuity. He told me he had already decided to blow the round on purpose on the last couple of holes, but, for him, that stunt was the icing on the cake. He said the only difficult part was forcing himself to upchuck by sticking his fingers down his throat."

"That man is something else," Jane said.

Augie laughed. "They don't call him the greatest con man who ever lived for nothing."

Chapter Sixteen

Boudreaux and Johnny were back on the golf course but kept their distance. Funaki, if it really was him, had nearly caught them spying on him from behind the thick trunk of a pecan tree. Johnny cursed himself for carelessly leaving his discarded, half-finished cigarette in the grass. From their new hiding place twenty yards away behind a stand of cedar trees, they watched Funaki peer curiously at the smoking cigarette butt on the ground, then glance around him. He looked apprehensive, even a little frightened.

"You and your dumb cigarettes, Johnny," Boudreaux said. "The sunlight reflecting off your cigarette lighter was probably what caught his attention."

"Sorry, Boudreaux," Johnny said, with a look of embarrassment on his face. "I wasn't thinking when I lit my cigarette."

Against Boudreaux's advice, Johnny had taken up the nasty habit several years ago. It was his way of dealing with post-war stress.

"What do you think he's doing here?" Johnny asked, as they watched Funaki and his caddie disappear around the bend of the tree-lined fairway.

"I don't know. Let's go ask Augie. I'm sure he'll be able to tell us something about our old friend."

"You can't be serious, Boudreaux," Augie said from behind the desk in his office. "I thought those animals were rounded up and imprisoned or executed after the war."

"The ones they caught were," Boudreaux said. "Funaki disappeared from the POW camp right after liberation day."

"That's right," added Johnny. "He was one of the few who escaped. He bragged about coming from a wealthy and powerful family, so it's likely he had the financial help to disappear. I'm sure it would have been easy for him to lay low somewhere. Even to have some surgery on his face to escape detection."

"Which brings us back to Johnny's question," Boudreaux said. "What's he doing here, of all places? If he's got that much influence, why not just return to Japan disguised as a common soldier with a new identity and start a new life?"

"Don't forget who lost the war, Boudreaux," Augie said. "The Japanese are bitter about the outcome and lay the blame on the military for the mess they found themselves in. Especially when they found out they were lied to about American soldiers being barbaric murderers and rapists. Our soldiers treated the civilians better than their own military did. I'm sure Funaki, being a defeated soldier, wouldn't have received a warm welcome upon his return. By the way, do you think he would recognize you two?"

"I don't think so," Johnny said. "The last time he saw us, we looked like walking skeletons."

"What do you know about him, Augie?" Boudreaux asked.

"He and his wife registered yesterday under the names of Arata and Sachi Oshiro. And I've got to tell you, she's quite a looker. She must be twenty years younger than him.

He didn't mention what he does for a living, but from the looks of the new Cadillac they arrived in and the fancy clothes they're wearing, they're not hurting for money."

"He didn't mention anything at all about where they're from or why they're here?" Boudreaux asked.

"No, but his car plates are from California. Could be just a little vacation."

"Out here?" Johnny asked incredulously. "With his dough, why cross the desert to visit a golf resort out in the middle of nowhere when he could afford to go anywhere in the country?"

Augie smiled as he leaned back in his chair and laced his fingers behind his head. "Boudreaux, tomorrow you'll have the opportunity to get answers to those questions and more."

"What do you mean?" Boudreaux asked.

"Mr. Oshiro told me his wife is interested in taking a few golf lessons. He said she thinks golf will be something they can share. He didn't seem too thrilled with the idea. I have a feeling he was just humoring her, that once she gets bored with it, she'll drop it."

"I could use the money," Boudreaux said. "What time did you tell her to meet me at the range?"

"Ten in the morning. Try to convince her to come every day. Her lesson fees might foot your entire trip to Corpus Christi."

Boudreaux was in a quandary. The man he hated and vowed vengeance upon had just showed up in his backyard after all these years, and that man wanted Boudreaux to give his wife golf lessons. His loathing for the Japanese had not diminished one bit, so he was apprehensive about how this meeting with his old foe's wife would affect him. If he hadn't needed the money, he would have refused to see her. Could he even speak to her without the burning hatred showing in his eyes? He would find out tomorrow morning.

Chapter Seventeen

Laughter filled the air on the driving range. It was nine-thirty a.m., and Boudreaux was teaching Mickey the basics and joys of golf. He hadn't planned on introducing Mickey to the game until he was a little more mature, but circumstances changed that.

The week before, Mickey had been sent home early from school for fighting. One of his classmates had called his mother a gimp, and Mickey retaliated by slamming the kid's head against the monkey bars.

In his frustration, upon arriving home Mickey had blamed his mother for the fight. "Why do you have to be so different from the other mothers?" he had yelled at her.

When Boudreaux heard about this from a tearful Jane, he found Mickey in his bedroom and dragged him by the collar out to the back yard for a little man-to-man talk.

"You little ingrate!" Boudreaux said, barely able to control his anger. "You think your mom asked to be different? Do you? So what if the other kids make fun of her? That's their problem, not yours."

Mickey sat on the backyard stoop and hung his head in shame. He knew he was wrong in hurting his mother like that, but his frustration had been building for a long time. That smart-mouthed kid wasn't the only one who had teased him about his mother. That day he just lost it and whaled into the kid. Still seething, he unfairly took it out on his mother when he got home.

"I'm sorry, Uncle Boudreaux. I didn't mean to hurt Mom. I couldn't help it. The other kids always make fun of her."

Boudreaux sat next to Mickey on the stoop. As tears rolled down the boy's cheeks, Boudreaux's voiced softened. "You know, Mickey, your mom's had it rough. Can you imagine what she must have put up with when she was your age? Being different? Then losing her husband in the war? She deserves better than that from you. She and your grandfather have worked their tails off to give you a better life than they had."

Boudreaux put a big hand under Mickey's chin and gently lifted it until their eyes met. Mickey was surprised to see tears in Boudreaux's eyes, too.

"Mickey, you're going to do two things for me. First, you're going to go inside and give your mom a big hug, tell her you're sorry and that you're proud of her. Tell her you love her and that you'll never hurt her again."

"Okay, Uncle Boudreaux," Mickey sniffed, wiping his nose on a dirty sleeve.

"Second, meet me tomorrow morning at eight on the driving range. If you're determined to beat someone, do it on a golf course, like a man."

"You really mean it?" Mickey said, as he leapt excitedly to his feet. "You're going to teach me to golf?"

"Yeah, I think it's about time. I was planning on waiting until you were a little older, but now is as good a time as any. Maybe golf will keep you so occupied you won't have time to worry about what others think of you and your family. Now, go on inside. I think someone's waiting for you."

After watching Mickey walk up the steps into the cabin to apologize to his mom, Boudreaux turned and headed back to his own cabin, wondering if his words had hit home. *Poor kid. No dad. Flawed mother. A grandfather who still harbors guilt over that fatal car accident years ago that took his wife and hurt his little girl. Mickey needs a father figure. I think I'm about the closest thing to a dad he'll ever have. Truth be told, I think I need him as much as he needs me.*

The next morning, Mickey's laughter rang out across the golf course from Boudreaux's clowning around. While he knew the importance of teaching Mickey the basics of the grip, stance, and swing, Boudreaux had decided to toss in a few comical, exaggerated swings as well. He purposely whiffed the ball occasionally and accidentally smacked the club into the ground a few times for good measure. To an observer, Boudreaux's antics must have seemed odd, but he was doing all this with a purpose—he was trying to make Mickey laugh and forget about his troubles for a while. Mickey knew this was all an act—he had watched Boudreaux enough to know he was an excellent golfer—and got a big kick out of it.

They were having so much fun, that Boudreaux lost track of the time and didn't see the petite, Asian woman watching them from a distance. It was fifteen minutes past ten, and Sachi Oshiro was having second thoughts about taking her first golf lesson.

Mickey stopped in his tracks and stared at the woman. Wondering what caught Mickey's attention, Boudreaux slowly turned around. His pulse quickened. *My God, she's beautiful!* he thought. Augie had said Funaki's wife was good-looking, but he hadn't expected to be captivated by such a striking woman. If Boudreaux hadn't needed the money so badly he would have told Augie he wasn't interested in meeting with her. But after seeing her, Boudreaux knew he would be willing to give her lessons free of charge.

Boudreaux had vowed that if he ever ran across Funaki, he would kill him. Now that he had the chance, he didn't know if he could do it—especially after meeting Funaki's wife. How would killing him affect her? Or their children, if they had any? In his rage, he hadn't thought about those things.

"Are you Boudreaux?" she asked, snapping him out of his reverie.

"Yes. You must be Mrs. Oshiro."

"Please, call me Sachi," she said in a flawless American accent.

"I'm sorry to keep you waiting. I was giving my friend, Mickey, a golf lesson and hadn't noticed the time."

She stared at him with beautiful, almond-shaped, azure eyes. *Those eyes,* Boudreaux thought. *Every Japanese person I encountered had dark brown eyes.* She was an anomaly—that rare Japanese woman with the sky-blue eyes of a Westerner.

Sachi grew uncomfortable with Boudreaux's prolonged gaze. She briefly lowered her eyes. "I was thinking of taking some golf lessons from you," she said, forcing herself to look up at Boudreaux. "But I think I might have made a mistake."

Boudreaux looked at Mickey for a second, and it suddenly dawned on him. She had mistaken his clowning around for ineptitude.

He smiled. "I can explain. We were just—"

"I can see you are busy," she interrupted. "I am sorry to have bothered you, Boudreaux. Have a nice day."

I can't let her leave now, Boudreaux thought, as she turned and started to walk away. Something stirred in Boudreaux's chest.

"Please, wait," he said, with a slight catch in his throat.

Sachi turned and looked at him with questioning eyes. Boudreaux walked over to her. A shiver went down his spine when he noticed a faint bruise under her left eye. Apparently, she had tried, unsuccessfully, to cover it with makeup, but Boudreaux had witnessed enough beatings to know a black eye when he saw one. Anger simmered under his calm exterior. *Funaki did that to her. There's no doubt in my mind.* For a beautiful woman to stay with a sadistic man like that, Boudreaux knew he had to have some sort of control over her. Perhaps he had rescued her from a life of poverty, or she had done something illegal, and he was blackmailing her. He had to find out.

He waved at the few cars scattered about the parking lot. "Which car is your husband's?" he asked.

"Excuse me?"

"Which car is your husband's?"

She had a puzzled look on her face, as she pointed to the far side of the lot. "The black Cadillac is my husband's car."

Boudreaux walked over to his thin, cloth golf bag lying on the grass and pulled out his adjustable club and two golf balls. He dropped them both on the grass and adjusted the club head to the angle of a pitching wedge. He took his stance and addressed the ball. With the perfect, fluid swing of a man who had spent years perfecting his game, Boudreaux sailed a beautiful, high-arching shot that hit the center of the Cadillac's hood, leaving a small dent the size of a dime.

"Do you think he would like a matching dent on the roof?" he asked, trying to mask his enjoyment at defacing his enemy's luxury car.

Her slow-spreading, beautiful smile melted Boudreaux's heart which, until this chance meeting, had forgotten what love was.

"I don't understand," she said. "With that little boy, you didn't seem to know what you were doing. But, it's obvious you do."

Boudreaux tossed the club and the other ball to Mickey, who put them back into the bag. "The first thing I try to do when I'm teaching young kids how to play golf is to establish rapport and gain their trust. The best way to do that is to make it, above all else, fun. What purpose would it serve for me to intimidate them from the start with a bunch of fancy shots they know they can't make? That approach would probably drive them away."

Boudreaux turned and looked at Mickey. "I'll see you later this evening if you like, Mickey. We can work on your putting." Boudreaux raised his eyebrows while giving a subtle tilting of his head. *Beat it, kid!* he thought.

"Okay, Uncle Boudreaux," Mickey said, taking the hint. Before he left, he gave Boudreaux a sly grin and rolled his eyes. He turned and ran to the grill to see if his mom needed any help.

"Nice boy," Sachi said.

"Mickey's a good kid, but he's had a lot of adversity to deal with in his short life. His self-esteem is in the basement. All that stuff you saw a while ago was just something I do to put him at ease. He's young. I can teach him the proper skills later when he's ready."

Sachi gave Boudreaux an understanding smile. She reached out and touched his cheek. Something in her touch kindled feelings in Boudreaux that he hadn't felt in a long time.

"I like you, Boudreaux," she said. "When do we start?"

"We already did," Boudreaux said, not sure if he was talking about golf lessons—or something else. Complex feelings swirled through his mind. He expected to hate this woman just as he had hated all Japanese since his capture. How could such a cruel race produce someone like Sachi? The local Japanese women he had encountered on his work details outside Camp Fukuoka #17 had cursed and spat on him. He was now experiencing an emotion much more powerful than hate for the beautiful woman with the azure eyes.

Chapter Eighteen

When Sachi arrived at the driving range the next morning, Boudreaux was already there, pounding long, straight drives with his adjustable club.

"Good morning, Boudreaux."

"Good morning, Sachi. Ready for your lesson?" Again, Boudreaux was mesmerized by her beauty.

"Yes, I'm ready."

Boudreaux put the club back into the golf bag and brought out a regulation 7 iron. When giving lessons, he never used the adjustable club. That was reserved for his own use.

"Before we begin, Sachi, would it be impolite of me to ask you a little bit about yourself?" Boudreaux was more interested in getting her to talk about her husband without arousing suspicion.

"No, Boudreaux. I don't mind." She told Boudreaux she and her husband were only staying a few days. Their plan was for her to occupy her time taking golf lessons every day while he was out on the golf course working on his game.

Boudreaux was pleased to hear that. It would give him time to get to know her a little better—he hadn't stopped thinking about her since he met her—and also give him the opportunity to pump her for more information about her husband.

"Augie mentioned you and your husband drove out here from California," Boudreaux said. "What made you choose such a desolate place as Whispering Hollows?"

"My husband has gotten it into his head that he wants to become a professional golfer in America. I think it's a ridiculous idea, but he believes that if he qualifies for the U.S. Open next month and does well, he'll have the chance to prove to the world that an Asian golfer can compete with American and British golfers."

Boudreaux stood motionless, an expression of disbelief on his face. He seemed not to notice the 7 iron slowly slipping from his fingers. Sachi laughed, mistaking the look on his face for one of amusement.

"I know. It sounds ridiculous, doesn't it? He entered the regional qualifying tournament in Corpus Christi next week. Since he heard such favorable things about this golf resort from some friends, he decided to visit here first to get in a little practice on a Texas course."

Boudreaux had a hard time processing what he had just heard. What were the odds of Funaki attempting to qualify for the same tournament as him and then showing up at Whispering Hollows the week before?

"Uh... no, not so ridiculous," Boudreaux stammered. "It's open to anyone who can come up with the fee. I was thinking of entering the qualifier myself."

"That's great, Boudreaux. You should meet my husband."

"That might not be such a good idea, Sachi."

"Why not?"

"I don't know how many golfers will be there, but only the top forty will advance to the U.S. Open. Your husband might not like your taking lessons from someone he'll be competing against. So please, don't mention it to him. If he asks who your instructor is, tell him it's some young kid named James."

The real reason he didn't want her to mention him to her husband was, even though Funaki probably wouldn't recognize his face, he might recognize his unusual name. Boudreaux wasn't quite ready to confront his nemesis. The right time would come for that.

Sachi walked over and bent down to pick up the 7 iron that Boudreaux had dropped. His throat tightened as he caught a faint scent of her perfume. *Simmer down, Boudreaux,* he thought to himself. *She's a married woman. An extremely attractive married woman. But still married.*

"That will be our little secret," she said with a playful tone in her voice. "Where do we start?"

As Boudreaux placed the club in her hands and showed her the proper grip, he snuck a peak at the bruise under her left eye. Enhanced by the bright morning sunlight, there was no doubt in his mind. Funaki was a wife beater.

They spent an enjoyable hour on the range going over the basics of the grip, stance, and swing. Sachi caught on fast. She was very graceful and had great hand-eye coordination. She moved like a trained dancer. Wherever she was from, it was obvious she had received sound training in dance or athletics. How did someone as talented as she was end up with a man like Funaki?

"Sachi, I know you and your husband are from California, but you're obviously Japanese. I don't mean to be rude, but I'm curious to know how you two ended up in California."

Sachi's face momentarily clouded over. Just as quickly, it brightened as she flashed a demure smile.

"We're both from Tokyo. Arata, my husband, was a successful industrialist before the war. I was his secretary. We fell in love, and he asked me to marry him. I would have been crazy to refuse such an offer. We were both thankful that the importance of his job kept him out of the military—and that terrible war.

"Despite his opposition to the war, he was at the mercy of a tyrannical military regime. His company provided weapons and supplies to the Japanese Army. After Japan's surrender, we both in shame decided to escape the devastation and misery the war brought our country. We came to America as soon as we could and settled in California."

Boudreaux nodded, pretending to understand. *She's lying. I can believe she was against the war, but she's lying to me about how they met. My guess is she latched onto him after the war for his money and a better life in America.*

"I hope America is everything you hoped it would be," Boudreaux said, trying to sound upbeat but feeling a sadness inside for this woman.

"Oh, it is," she said.

"I must admit I'm impressed with how well you speak English."

"Arata and I both learned some English in school when we were young. Later, the international demands of his job required we both become proficient in the language."

Boudreaux looked pensive for a few moments before he spoke. "It looks like our time is up, Sachi. Same time tomorrow?"

"I'll be here."

After they said their goodbyes, Boudreaux placed the 7 iron in his golf bag and returned to his cabin. His mind swirled with possible scenarios. *How did they really meet? Funaki might have been an industrialist before and after the war, but he sure wasn't one during the war.* And the answers she gave sounded scripted, as if Funaki had coached her on what to say if anyone asked too many questions about their past.

Boudreaux didn't want to hurt Sachi, but he needed to do something. He was experiencing strong feelings for this mysterious woman. He needed to find a way to get her away from Funaki before it was too late. The man was a sadistic murderer. Tomorrow he would attempt to pry more information from Sachi without alarming her.

Jeez, Boudreaux. What are you getting yourself into?

✕
Chapter Nineteen

Boudreaux awoke the next morning in anticipation of the morning session with Sachi. He had dreamt of her. He was back in Camp Fukuoka #17, sitting on his bunk nursing bruises from his latest beating from Captain Funaki.

"Boudreaux," a soft feminine voice called from outside the small window above his head. A pair of beautiful, azure eyes stared at him from the blackness.

"It's Sachi, Boudreaux," she whispered. "You must come with me. I can save you." There was a sadness in her voice. "He will kill you. I can save you if you come with me."

In a trance, Boudreaux stood on his bunk and climbed out the window. She took his hand in hers, and they started to run.

"Stop, or I will shoot you!" a familiar voice yelled.

Boudreaux and Sachi stopped and turned. Funaki raised his rifle, just as Sachi stepped in front of Boudreaux. As her body slipped to the cold, blood-stained ground, Sachi looked deep into Boudreaux's eyes. "I can still save you, Boudreaux, if you follow me."

Captain Funaki laughed, then turned and walked away. Boudreaux sat on the ground, cradling the dying woman's head in his lap.

"Sachi!" Boudreaux cried, as he caressed her face. "Don't leave me."

"Boudreaux, wake up!"

Boudreaux bolted upright in his bed. "Huh?" he asked, slowly coming out his bizarre dream.

"You were having a nightmare. You kept yelling Sachi's name. Are you okay?"

"Yeah, I'm okay, Johnny." Boudreaux rubbed his eyes. "I was dreaming I was back in Japan. Sachi was trying to save me."

Johnny smiled. "Uh oh. Looks like someone's been bitten by the bug."

Boudreaux pushed Johnny away and sat up. "Don't even think that, Johnny. She's married to our worst enemy."

"I haven't forgotten that. I hope you don't either."

"Go to bed, Johnny," Boudreaux said, as he lay back and pulled the covers up over his head. "We can talk about this later."

Johnny was as surprised as Boudreaux was to learn of Funaki's plans to attempt to qualify for the U.S. Open and later join the professional ranks. They had discussed ways to exact their revenge on Funaki, now that they had found him. Since Funaki didn't know they were on to him, they knew they had the element of surprise and could bide their time.

Boudreaux found Sachi waiting for him on the range later in the morning. She was even more beautiful than he had remembered. She wore stylish, white slacks with a sleeveless aquamarine blouse. Apparently, Sachi spared no expense when it came to her attire. She looked splendid, and Boudreaux found it difficult to keep his mind on the golf lesson.

He noticed that the bruise under her left eye had lightened a bit, but he detected reddish marks on her wrists that weren't there yesterday. *That maniac is still at it,* he thought.

I've got to say something. After twenty minutes of working on Sachi's swing mechanics, Boudreaux decided he'd waited long enough.

"Sachi, how well do you know your husband?"

"That's a strange question, Boudreaux. Why do you ask?"

In response, he boldly, but gently, touched the bruise under her eye. Sachi recoiled in surprise. Boudreaux leaned down and took both her wrists in his.

"These marks on your wrist weren't there yesterday," he said as she pulled her arms away from him. "And please don't tell me you got that bruise under your eye walking into a door."

"You're very impertinent, Boudreaux. I came here for golf lessons, not the third degree. And why are you so interested in my husband?"

"I apologize, Sachi," Boudreaux said as he lowered his head. After a moment of silence, he raised his head and looked earnestly into her eyes. "You lied about working for your husband during the war."

"How would you know?" she asked with a fire in her eyes he hadn't noticed before.

Boudreaux was torn between grabbing her by the shoulders and shaking her or taking her in his arms and kissing her. He did neither.

"I know because Johnny and I were with your husband during the war—and we sure weren't his secretaries."

A veil of guilt clouded Sachi's beautiful, azure eyes. She appeared stunned, her mouth open but not saying anything for several moments.

"What are you talking about, Boudreaux?" she finally asked in a voice that was barely audible.

"Johnny, who you might have seen limping around the course, and I were in the Army during the war. We were captured by Japanese soldiers and spent over three years as guests of the Emperor. We were prisoners of war. We spent the last seven months in a place called Camp Fukuoka #17 near Japan's west coast. Your *industrialist* husband was the camp commander and went by the name of Akio Funaki. He was directly responsible for the deaths and beatings of hundreds of prisoners of war. Johnny and I were regular targets of his brutality."

Sachi stared at Boudreaux in disbelief. She was at a loss for words.

"You lied, Sachi. Why? Did you know nothing about his past?"

Tears filled Sachi's eyes. "Yes, Boudreaux, I did lie about working for him." Sachi walked over to a wooden bench nearby and sat down. She stared off into the distance.

Boudreaux felt a twinge of guilt for calling her a liar, but he needed to know the truth. He cared for her and wanted to protect her, but he couldn't do that if she lied to him. He sat next to her, his left knee touching hers. He was glad she didn't scoot away from him.

"We met after the war," she began. "He was an industrialist like I said. I had no idea what he did during the war. We were introduced by a mutual friend, and after seeing each other for a few months, he said he loved me and asked me to marry him."

"Were you in love with him?"

"I told him I was, but I wasn't. I came from a poor family, Boudreaux. My parents were killed in the war and left me with nothing. When he asked me to marry him, I thought that would be my way to a better life. When he told me of his plans to move to America, I was thrilled."

"You weren't curious about what he did during the war?"

"I wondered, but I was too afraid to ask. I was in a dream world, Boudreaux. He said he was from a wealthy family, so I figured his family's money and influence had helped him escape serving in the military."

"You don't believe me, do you, Sachi? About his being our camp commander."

"I don't know what to believe." She looked down at her wrists. "He's a cruel man, Boudreaux. I never would have married him if I had known he would treat me so badly. But what can I do? And how can you be sure my husband was your camp commander? That was a long time ago."

She looked into Boudreaux's eyes with a sadness that broke his heart. He wanted to hold her, to comfort her, to tell her that everything would be all right. Instead, he stood, walked a few steps away and picked at the bark of a nearby crape myrtle.

"It looks like he might have had some surgery to alter his facial features, but I'll never forget your husband's evil eyes. Johnny and I watched him on the course the other day. There's no mistake, Sachi. It's him. I can prove it to you, if you still don't believe me."

"How are you going to do that?"

"I'll need your help. Tonight, when you are having dinner, I want you to say something to him. Then watch his response very closely."

"What do I say?"

"Tell him you met an interesting man today in the pro shop. That he walked over and introduced himself as Budo.

Tell your husband you responded by saying, 'Budo, what kind of crazy name is that?' It's important that you say it exactly that way. Then look deeply into your husband's eyes. By his response, you'll know if I'm telling you the truth or not."

"Okay, Boudreaux. That sounds like a strange request, but I'll do it."

Boudreaux changed the subject by giving her a few more pointers on hitting the golf ball. He didn't want to overwhelm Sachi or scare her off with their discussion of her husband. When their time was up, Boudreaux slid the 7 iron into the golf bag.

"I'll see you tomorrow morning at 9:00, Sachi. Don't forget what we discussed."

"I won't, Boudreaux," Sachi said, as she turned and walked away in the direction of her cabin.

Boudreaux watched her until she was out of sight.

Chapter Twenty

Boudreaux paced nervously as he waited for Sachi to show up the next morning. She arrived promptly at 9:00 with a confused, faraway look on her face.

"Well?" Boudreaux asked, after waiting several minutes for her to say something. "What happened?"

"I believe you, Boudreaux," Sachi said, looking at the ground. "I said exactly what you told me to say."

"What was his response?"

Sachi raised her head and looked at Boudreaux for a long moment. "He looked like he had seen a ghost. His dropped his wine glass on the table. It broke and wine went everywhere. He barely noticed. I've never seen him like that."

"What then?"

"He demanded I describe the man to him. I told him it was just an old, fat man. He seemed relieved at first, but he still looked a little scared. I asked him why he was so upset. He just brushed it off, saying he doesn't like strange men talking to his wife."

"You need to leave him, Sachi. He's no good. You deserve better."

"Boudreaux, he's my husband. What can I do? I have no money of my own and no other family. I can't go back to Japan. In my culture, a wife doesn't just leave her husband without being disgraced. You must understand. There's nothing I can do."

Boudreaux didn't know what to say. He was beginning to have strong feelings for her and wanted to help her, but he didn't know how. He had vowed to kill Funaki if he ever found him, but, if he did, what would happen to Sachi?

"I understand. Believe me, I know how it feels to have someone else control your life. If you ever need me, I'll be here. I know I shouldn't be telling a married woman this, but I really like you, Sachi. If I hear of him hurting you again, I'm coming after him."

Sachi placed a smooth hand on Boudreaux's cheek. "You're very kind, Boudreaux. I wish my husband were more like you."

Boudreaux blushed. He didn't know how to respond. "Just be careful. I know you feel you can't escape from him, but there's always a way."

"I must go, Boudreaux," Sachi said, as she impulsively stood on her toes and kissed Boudreaux on the cheek. "I don't think I can handle this lesson now. I'm too upset. Can I see you tomorrow at nine?"

"I'll be waiting," Boudreaux said. He gingerly touched his cheek where she had just kissed him.

As he watched her walk away, Boudreaux felt his heart pounding in his chest. *I'll be waiting*, Boudreaux thought, unsure if he was referring to tomorrow's golf lesson or something else. Time would tell.

Chapter Twenty-One

Boudreaux sat quietly in the back seat of Augie's Studebaker. He tried to take his mind off Sachi by fiddling with his adjustable club. Johnny sat next to him, watching the flat south Texas landscape roll by. Neither one had said more than a dozen words since leaving Whispering Hollows.

It was a typical hot, south Texas day in late May. The next day, Saturday, was Boudreaux's make-or-break day. Tomorrow night, he would find out if he was headed to the 1949 United States Open in Medinah, Illinois.

"When are we going to the beach?" asked an excited Mickey from the front seat.

Jane momentarily took her right hand off the wheel long enough to tousle his unkempt hair.

"We'll go the beach Sunday morning, Mickey," she said. "You'll have all day to play in the water."

"Can't we go today?"

"No. Your Uncle Boudreaux needs to go straight to the golf course to check in and find out what he needs to do. Tonight we're just going to have dinner and relax. Boudreaux and Johnny have a lot on their minds right now."

If Boudreaux was nervous, he didn't show it. He absent-mindedly adjusted his club, starting with the putter setting up through all angle settings to the wedge, after which he re-adjusted it in reverse order. He had cleaned and oiled the lever and the gear teeth to make sure everything was in tiptop condition. Satisfied with his efforts, he laid the club aside. He patted Johnny on the knee.

"How are you doing, Johnny?"

Johnny turned his gaze from the seemingly endless succession of cotton fields to Boudreaux.

"Okay, I guess. A little nervous."

"You'll be fine, Johnny. The Oso Rojo course is pretty flat. You shouldn't have much trouble getting around."

Johnny looked out the window again, a faraway look in his eyes, as if the cotton fields were clouds and he was searching for something in their midst.

"What's eating you, Johnny? You're awful quiet. I thought you'd be more excited about this trip."

Johnny turned back to Boudreaux with a look of despair in his eyes that Boudreaux had never seen before. *Something's wrong,* Boudreaux thought. He decided it was better to keep silent and wait for Johnny to say something.

"I got a letter from my folks yesterday. It's about my little brother. The one who went missing in Malaysia."

Boudreaux waited for Johnny to continue.

"They found his remains in a mass grave at one of those POW camps. They identified him by his dog tags."

"I'm sorry, Johnny," Boudreaux said, putting a hand on his friend's shoulder.

Johnny lowered his head and brought his hands to his face. His shoulders heaved. Mickey looked back over the front seat curiously at Johnny's expression of grief. Boudreaux looked sternly at Mickey and shook his head slightly. He turned an index finger in a circular motion, an indication for Mickey to turn around. Mickey silently obeyed and scrunched down in his seat, understanding there were times it was wise to mind your own business.

By the time they reached the Oso Rojo clubhouse, Johnny had collected himself and gave no indication of his grief. After Boudreaux and Johnny checked in with the tournament director and paid the entry fee, the four of them stopped in the club grill for lunch. Later, they strolled around the meandering cart paths, checking out the layout of the course.

The beautiful, sub-tropical Oso Rojo Golf Course, with its fragrant pink and white oleander shrubs and majestic palm trees lining the fairways, was several miles northwest of downtown Corpus Christi. There weren't many trees to contend with, but the constant breeze coming off the Gulf of Mexico was going to be a huge factor. Boudreaux figured he could handle the breeze since he was used to playing the windy courses of central Texas.

They all spent the night in a cheap motor court just off the highway a mile from downtown. Jane took the only bed while Boudreaux and Johnny slept on blankets on the floor and Mickey curled up on the small couch.

Boudreaux and Johnny showed up at the clubhouse early Saturday morning to prepare for their 9 a.m. tee time for the Open qualifier, which consisted of two consecutive eighteen-hole rounds. It would be stroke play, and the top forty players would advance to the Open, which would be held in two weeks.

Boudreaux felt a stab of repulsion when he saw Funaki on the practice tee. He fervently wished Funaki would fall flat on his face, but after observing his superb ball-striking earlier at Whispering Hollows, he knew it was likely Funaki would breeze his way into the Open. *That's okay. It will just give me more time to plan my vengeance. It might also give me another opportunity to see Sachi.*

Boudreaux played well enough to place in the top twenty after eighteen holes. With Jane and Mickey in the gallery cheering him on, the round was uneventful except for the curious stares Boudreaux and Johnny received from the other players and spectators, who were fascinated by the sight of Johnny carrying the single club in its slim golf bag. Many scratched their heads in amusement, probably wondering if this was some sort of publicity stunt.

That is, until they saw how well Boudreaux controlled his shots. Their doubtful stares soon turned to looks of respect.

The only unusual episode occurred midway through the second round, when Boudreaux passed close to Funaki playing a fairway in the opposite direction. Sachi was following twenty yards behind her husband when she spotted Boudreaux and waved excitedly. Funaki stopped and peered closely at Boudreaux and Johnny for a few moments, as if he recognized them. He then turned back to his game.

Boudreaux wasn't sure if Funaki recognized them from their home course or, worse, from the POW camp. He was alarmed when Funaki abruptly turned and snapped his fingers, then broke into a broad smile.

"Hey. You're from Whispering Hollows, right?"

Boudreaux and Johnny nodded and smiled weakly but kept moving. *He doesn't recognize us from the camp,* Boudreau thought with relief.

"I guess he thinks we're club members back home," Boudreaux said to Johnny.

"For a second there, I thought he was on to us," Johnny said.

"Just stay away from him, Johnny. We don't want to push our luck. It hasn't been that long. I'll confront him with the truth when the time is right."

A few holes later, Boudreaux and Funaki crossed paths again. This time Funaki didn't notice Boudreaux, but Sachi did. She was standing under a tall sago palm with her arms crossed, pretending to watch her husband line up his shot, but out of the corner of her eye, she was watching Boudreaux.

When their eyes met, Boudreaux couldn't stop the exhilarating feeling that washed over him. He suddenly got a crazy—but potentially costly—idea. He was confident he was far enough ahead in the standings to risk losing a few shots to execute his risky plan.

Boudreaux had a clear, two-hundred-yard, long iron shot to the green. To his left, in the other fairway, Funaki was surveying his approach shot and looking around, checking the swirling wind conditions. Boudreaux waited until Funaki's back was to him then made eye contact with Sachi.

He pointed the index and middle fingers of his right hand to his eyes, then, quickly, reversed his hand so he was pointing the same two fingers to Funaki. Sachi cocked her head to one side in confusion.

Boudreaux addressed his ball and took a stance aiming at the green, but suddenly closed the club face forty-five degrees.

"Hey, Boudreaux! What the heck are you doing?" Johnny asked, alarmed by Boudreaux's obvious, last minute club face error.

"Shut up and watch, Johnny!" Boudreaux hissed as he drew the club back.

As Johnny shook his head in exasperation, the sharply angled club head's impact with the ball sent it caroming in a low, left trajectory in Funaki's direction. After a couple of seconds, it struck Funaki's butt dead center, sending him diving to the ground in pain.

"Fore!" Boudreaux yelled, after the damage was done. He stole a look at Sachi, who was looking at him and trying to stifle her laughter. He winked, then ran over to where Funaki laid sprawled on the ground.

"Oh, my God!" he said, helping the bewildered man to his feet. "I'm terribly sorry, sir. I must have shanked it. Are you okay?"

"Yes, I'm okay," an embarrassed Funaki said, as he brushed himself off and rubbed his behind. "So, we meet again. I don't know how you made it this far, hitting wild shots like that."

"It won't happen again, sir," Boudreaux said, as he looked over Funaki's shoulder at Sachi.

Luckily, Funaki couldn't see her, for she was still doubled over in laughter.

"Good luck with your round, sir," Boudreaux said as Funaki turned and limped back to his ball.

Boudreaux walked over to his ball, lying in the middle of the other fairway, set the club to a 7 iron and calmly hit it to within two feet of the pin for an easy tap-in for a par.

As Boudreaux predicted, both he and Funaki advanced to the prestigious United States Open Championship. Boudreaux finished fourth and Funaki finished seventh. After celebrating with some cold beers (and root beer) in the grill, Boudreaux, Johnny, Jane, and Mickey headed back to the motor court.

"I can't believe you're in the Open," Johnny said. "All that work finally paid off."

"You mean we're in the Open, Johnny. I couldn't have done it without you."

"What now?" Johnny asked.

"Monday, we make reservations for our week in Medinah. I hope Augie makes good on his promise to help with the expenses."

"It was nice of him to offer to let you borrow his car again for the trip," Jane said.

"That man has done an awful lot for us, Jane," Boudreaux said. "I hope we can pay your dad back someday."

"Just win the U.S. Open with that club he gave you. That will be enough. If you boys want to go to the beach tomorrow, we'd better hit the sack."

Mickey didn't need prompting. He was under the couch covers in five seconds flat.

"I can't wait to see my girlfriends tomorrow," he said, peeking mischievously over the top of his blanket.

Boudreaux and Johnny gave each other puzzled looks, while Jane smiled knowingly and shook her head.

Chapter Twenty-Two

Getting to Port Aransas on Mustang Island involved a thirty-mile drive westward around the top of Corpus Christi Bay. They drove through the small towns of Portland and Gregory to the coastal town of Aransas Pass. From there, after paying a one-dollar toll, they traveled on an old, rickety, wooden, asphalt-covered railroad bed to the eastern tip of Harbor Island. Before the railroad bed was covered in asphalt in 1930, the short railway flatcars had been the only means of transporting cars the five miles to the ferry landing on Harbor Island.

"That's Port Aransas on the other side of the channel," Jane said, pointing to a cluster of wooden buildings.

"And just how do we get there?" Johnny asked, shielding his eyes from the bright glare reflecting off the choppy water. "Swim?"

"One of my girlfriends will be here any minute to pick us up and take us over," Mickey said, scanning the channel.

Boudreaux and Johnny exchanged doubtful glances, while Johnny twirled an index finger in circles next to his temple.

"Look! Here comes one now," Mickey shouted excitedly. "Say hello to the Nellie B."

Johnny looked on in wonderment as a weather-beaten ferry eased up to the wooden landing. Boudreaux had ridden the ferries many times before, but was amused at Mickey's girlfriend reference. The rubber bumpers of the landing creaked against the bow of the ferry as the boarding ramp was hydraulically adjusted to the level of the deck.

"That's just one of my girls," Mickey said proudly. "Those two ferries out there are my other sweeties," he said pointing to the middle of the channel.

The one approaching the landing had the name "Estella" painted on her hull. The one heading across the channel away from them with a full load of cars had the name "Ruby" on her hull.

"Those are your girlfriends," Johnny said, more as a statement than a question.

"Well, yeah," Mickey said. "You didn't think I meant real girls, did you? I'm only eight years old, you know."

Boudreaux and Johnny laughed.

"Mickey, you're something else," Boudreaux said, grabbing the boy in an affectionate headlock and rubbing a knuckle into his mass of sandy-colored hair.

"The dollar toll I paid back in Aransas Pass was for the ferry ride," Jane said.

"There's no other way to get to Mustang Island?" Johnny asked.

"No," said Boudreaux. "Not right now. Years ago, visitors could drive from Flour Bluff just south of Corpus Christi over the Don Patricio Causeway to the northern tip of Padre Island. From there they would cross a small bridge to the southern end of Mustang Island, then drive seventeen miles north up the beach to Port Aransas."

"What happened?" Johnny asked.

"In '33 a hurricane destroyed the causeway. A new one is being built, but won't be finished until next year. So, unless you take a boat, the only way to get there is across the channel on one of these ferries."

Boudreaux and Johnny looked over the side as the ferry chugged away from the landing.

"I think I like this way better," Johnny said, with a look of contentment on his face.

"Me, too," Mickey yelled, as he chased away a couple of seagulls trying to perch on the hood of their car. "I hope they never finish that old causeway. I think my girlfriends would all die of broken hearts if I quit coming this way."

Boudreaux found the steady thrum of the big diesel engine and the gentle rocking of the ferry to be very relaxing. His thoughts turned to Sachi. He smiled as he thought of the way she laughed hysterically when his errant fairway shot smacked her husband in the butt.

This pleasant memory was interrupted when a blast of salt spray splashed across the ferry's gunwale and hit him in the face. He put an arm around Mickey's shoulder, as they both perused the horizon. "Cherish days like this, Mickey. It's memories of times like these that will see you through just about anything that life throws at you."

"What do you mean, Uncle Boudreaux?"

"Never mind," Boudreaux said, squeezing Mickey's neck gently. "I was just thinking out loud." *I hope to God Mickey never has to see the things his dad, grandpa, Johnny, and I have seen.*

After the ten-minute ride across the channel, they disembarked from the Nellie B. and Jane drove the car up the loading ramp. She then headed down Cotter Avenue for another mile to Tarpon Street, passing several small marinas on the left and a few sun-bleached buildings on the right.

"Our trip to Port Aransas wouldn't be complete without first stopping at Shorty's for a cold one," Jane said as she turned left on Tarpon Street. She continued down the sandy, crushed-shell road for another two hundred feet then turned left and stopped in front of a wooden structure with a covered porch.

"A nice lady named Gladys Fowler, who I've become good friends with, opened up this beer joint in '46. It's one of my favorite stops. It's where I catch up on the local gossip and hear the latest fishing stories. She likes it when I drop by, because most of her other customers are smelly old fishermen."

"If they've got cold beer, it's already on my hit list," Johnny said. "Drinks are on me."

"I've got to warn you, though," Jane said. "There's an old coot who works here who will talk your ear off if you let him."

"Thanks for the warning," Boudreaux said as they climbed the wooden steps and entered the building.

Once inside, they sat on tall stools at the rough, cedar-plank bar. A nice-looking, tiny, middle-aged woman approached them and extended her arms in greeting.

"Jane, good to see you again," she said, grabbing Jane in a tight embrace.

"Hi, Gladys. You remember Mickey," Jane said looking over at her son.

"Yeah, I remember that little squirt," Gladys said, playfully tickling Mickey in the stomach.

"I'm not a little squirt," a defensive Mickey said with a phony pout on his face. "I've grown two inches since last summer."

"Oh, I can see that. Now you're a big squirt."

Mickey climbed up on his stool and gave his mother's friend a friendly hug. It was obvious they were crazy about each other.

"Gladys, meet Boudreaux and Johnny," Jane said. "They're good friends of mine."

"Pleasure to meet you, Boudreaux, Johnny."

"Nice to meet you, Gladys," Boudreaux said, standing and extending his hand.

"The pleasure's all mine, Gladys," Johnny said, also standing and holding out his hand.

"Please, call me Shorty. I think Jane's the only one who knows my real name around here. Y'all look like you could use a couple of cold brews."

"We just have time for one round, Gladys," Jane said. "We'll be back later, though. How have you been?"

"Not bad. Still trying to stay above water, literally and figuratively. Hurricane season's just around the corner, you know. Seems like every time one blows through the island, we lose a few more landmarks."

"Your place looks sturdy. I'm sure it'll weather any storms that blow through here. Speaking of blowhards, is Willie still working here?"

Gladys grinned. "He's still here. He works later this evening. He always looks forward to seeing you and Mickey. You need to introduce him to your friends."

"I warned them about his gift for gab."

"Yeah, he does have that, but he's still a heck of a nice guy, and he's the best bartender I've ever had." She turned and waved an arm at the walls of the bar. "He's also known for being a gifted sketch artist."

"She's right," Jane said.

Gladys served them their beers and excused herself, promising to bring Jane up to speed on the latest gossip later.

"What does Willie sketch?" asked Boudreaux.

"He likes to do quick portraits of the more interesting-looking people who come in here and add them to his collection on the walls. He's somewhat of a dreamer who thinks he'll be discovered someday by a famous art connoisseur. Everyone around here just humors him, telling him not to give up."

"Nothing wrong with that," Johnny said.

"He's been waiting to be discovered for over twenty years," Jane said. "He just drifted around the island until Gladys, out of the goodness of her heart, hired him. Gladys made a wise decision. He's been good for business. The customers love him."

Boudreaux was impressed with the myriad collection of portraits lining the bar's wood-paneled walls. "Man, these are really good. What's he doing tending bar here? He should be doing art exhibits around the country."

"He's a veteran of the Great War," Jane said. "Like Dad, he still has some personal demons from those days to deal with. He came down here from San Antonio shortly after the war ended to get away from it all. Despite his proclaimed desire to be discovered, when someone does offer to help him, he shies away. He probably knows he's not ready for the limelight or the fame. So he stays here and does his sketches. I think it's his form of therapy."

"I can understand that," Boudreaux said. "I've been down that road myself."

"One curious thing about him, though," Jane said, in a low voice. "He claims to have a sixth sense and only draws what he sees, good or bad. Not what others necessarily see. Some customers have taken offense at their likenesses. Willie just shrugs it off and ignores their comments."

"Sounds kind of spooky to me," Johnny said.

"If he asks if it's okay to sketch you and Johnny, you might want to think on it before you answer," Jane said. "Some say he can see right into your soul and show you things about yourself you may not want to see."

"Are you and Mickey up there anywhere?" Boudreaux asked, looking around.

Jane pointed to a far corner of the bar. "We're back there, if you'd care to take a look."

Boudreaux and Johnny carried their drinks to where Jane had pointed. After finding their portraits, Boudreaux and Johnny stood silently as they gazed upon the finely detailed drawings.

The standout feature of Jane's portrait was her fully-developed arms. The faint image of a young woman with features similar to Jane's was barely discernible to Jane's left. To Boudreaux's astonishment, she was holding Jane's left hand.

Mickey's portrait showed a smiling boy who appeared to be about six years old wearing a pirate's hat. A beautiful, green parrot was perched on his left shoulder. Barely visible over his right shoulder was a faint image of the same woman who appeared in Jane's portrait. Her left hand was resting lightly on Mickey's shoulder. She was kissing him on the cheek.

Boudreaux and Johnny returned to their stools where Jane and Mickey were waiting with expectant looks on their faces.

"Did you two recognize my mother?" Jane asked. "I'm sure you've both seen her picture on Dad's desk."

"We did," Boudreaux said, Johnny nodding his head in agreement.

"I don't remember much about her, but I recognized her face. Willie never met my mother. I never told him she was dead. When he showed me the finished drawing, I broke down. Willie then took my hand in his. 'It's all right,' he said. 'Your mother's doing just fine. She says she loves you and Mickey very much and is proud of you both. She misses you. I promise, you will see her again, Jane.'"

Mickey laid his head against his mother's arm and looked at Boudreaux with a peaceful look in his eyes. "Willie said my grandma is my guardian angel. He told me he saw her kiss me while he was drawing me."

"I believe you, little man," Boudreaux said, affectionately tousling Mickey's hair. "We could all use a guardian angel."

"Hurry up and finish those beers," Mickey said, suddenly jumping off his stool. "I want to get to the beach before it gets too late."

They finished their drinks and told Gladys to save them some cold ones for later that afternoon when they would return for a bite to eat. After saying goodbye, they piled into the car and headed south on Alister Street. They continued for one mile then took a left on Avenue G. Four blocks down on the left, Jane pointed out the Rock Cottages Motor Court.

"That's where Mickey and I like to stay when we come down for the weekend. It's a well-known landmark, plus it's reasonable and a short walk to the beach. It seems to be about the only place that's immune to the hurricanes. That's probably because it's made with rocks brought down from a quarry in San Antonio."

"Looks like it could withstand about anything," Boudreaux observed.

"It was built by the famous fishing guide, Barney Farley, before World War II to house his many fishing clients," Jane said. "Barney's fishing guide business was a big boost to the local economy. He even took President Roosevelt out tarpon fishing on one of his family's famous Farley boats back in '37."

"I'm impressed," Boudreaux said. "What do you say we come back here soon and do some fishing, Johnny?"

"Count me in. We'd better count Mickey in too," he said, eyeing a bright-eyed Mickey, "or we'll never hear the end of it."

They continued driving down the road to the beach access, where Jane parked the car midway between the dunes and the surf. They climbed out of the car and ducked behind the dunes to change into their swimsuits.

"All right," Boudreaux yelled, coming out from behind a dune. "Last one in is a rotten... Hey, where's Mickey?" he asked, looking at Jane and Johnny standing next to the car.

Jane just smiled and pointed an index finger down the beach. "Guess."

There, a hundred yards down the beach, all that was visible of Mickey was a cloud of sand trailing behind a boy who appeared as all knees and elbows whooping and hollering.

A few seconds later, Mickey turned right and made a beeline to the water.

"I don't think I know of anyone who likes the beach as much as that kid does," Boudreaux said, suddenly bolting in a dead run after Mickey. "Except for me!" he yelled over his shoulder.

"Hey, wait for me!" Johnny answered, his clumsy gait making it difficult for him to keep up.

His lagging behind didn't dampen his spirits one bit. As soon as he hit the water, he dove in and caught up with Boudreaux and Mickey, who were playfully splashing and dunking each other. Jane went off by herself and dove into the swirling surf and swam out past the second sandbar, where she floated lazily on her back, inhaling the pure, salt air.

Later, as the sun began to set behind the dunes covered in sea oats, morning glories, and coastal bluestem grass, it cast jagged shadows across the beach. The exhausted group of best friends sat contentedly on their towels watching hopeful fishermen dangling their lines off the South Pier just a short distance down the beach.

"I wish we could live down here all the time," Mickey said, poking a stick at a cornered sand crab that was brandishing its tiny claws in defiance.

"Do good in school, get a good job, and save your money, Mickey," Boudreaux said, "and you can live anywhere you want. This place is nice to visit a couple of times a year, but I'll take the Texas Hill Country any old day."

"That goes double for me," Johnny said. "At least up there, you don't have to worry about bullies kicking sand in your face."

With that, he leapt to his feet and kicked up a cloud of sand at a surprised Mickey.

"You're in for it now, Uncle Johnny!" Mickey laughed, as he tried, a second too late, to roll out of the way. "I hate bullies!"

He jumped up and chased a cackling Johnny down the beach until he caught up and brought him down. They rolled around like a couple of seagulls fighting over a shrimp, emitting fits of laughter until they collapsed on the sand.

Johnny stood. "We'd better rinse off. We'll be leaving soon."

He pulled Mickey to his feet, after which they both jumped into the still warm water.

Jane stood and shook off her towel. "Johnny and Mickey are crazy about each other," she said. "I hope Johnny has kids of his own someday. He'd make a terrific father. So would you, Boudreaux."

Boudreaux laughed. "I already have Johnny and Mickey."

"Yeah, but you've got room in your heart for a few more. What do you say we go back to Shorty's for some burgers and beer before we head home?"

"I'm in," Boudreaux said, standing and shaking off his towel. "I'm starved."

They signaled for Johnny and Mickey to come out of the water. After changing into their clothes, they drove the short distance to Shorty's.

Fifteen minutes later, they were seated at the bar, Mickey drinking a root beer and the others sipping cold beers. Willie, the bartender/artist, manned the counter. He was a wiry, older man with thinning, gray hair and a well-maintained goatee.

His face had the weathered look of a man who had spent years in the sun.

While they were waiting for their food to arrive, Willie entertained them with stale jokes and witty observations of the world at large. Boudreaux and Johnny found he was everything Jane had warned them about. In spite of that, he was immensely likeable. They took to him immediately.

"Hey, Johnny," Boudreaux whispered to his friend, when Willie was out of earshot. "Let's ask him if he'll sketch our portraits. That will allow future customers to see the two handsomest men from the Texas Hill Country."

Jane and Mickey looked at each other and rolled their eyes.

"I'll drink to that, Boudreaux," Johnny said, with a wink as he took a long, slow draw of his beer.

"Don't forget what I said," Jane said. "He draws what he sees. Don't take offense if you don't like what you see."

"We'll take our chances," Boudreaux said. "We've seen a lot of bad things in our life. I'm sure we can handle a silly portrait. Right, Johnny?"

"That's right, Boudreaux," Johnny said.

"Willie," Jane said. "These two handsome devils want to know if you'll add their faces to your wall collection. Do you have the time?"

"I always have time for my friends," Willie said, with a big smile. "New and old. Let me get my stuff."

Willie ducked back into the storeroom and retrieved a flimsy, wooden easel, two sheets of blank drawing paper and some freshly sharpened pencils. He moved aside a glass jar that had a stenciled label reading *Support your local intellectual. Will pontificate for tips.* He set up the easel in front of Johnny.

While Willie was studying Johnny's face, Mickey's attention was drawn to the label on the jar. "Mom," he whispered. "What does pontificate mean?"

Jane leaned over so no one else could hear. "It means to pretend to know what you're talking about, when, in fact, you don't know jack." They both laughed under their breath, hoping Willie wouldn't hear them. They didn't want to hurt his feelings.

"What's my best side, Boudreaux?" Johnny joked as he posed in various positions.

"If you want Willie to draw your best side, maybe you should stand on your head," Boudreaux said, taking a sip of his beer.

"Har-de-har-har," Johnny countered. "You're just jealous."

Willie told Johnny to look straight ahead, so he could look into his eyes. Willie slowly rubbed his bristly chin for a few minutes as if he was uncertain as to whether he should proceed.

"I draw what I see, Johnny," Willie said, a sadness darkening his eyes. "Just to let you know."

"Go ahead, Willie. I'm curious to know what you see."

For the next ten minutes, Johnny sat motionless, while Willie wove his magic. When he was done, he laid his pencil down and turned the easel around for all to see. Johnny gasped as he brought a trembling hand to his mouth. Tears formed in the corners of his eyes. There was no doubt in his mind that Willie was, indeed, someone very special.

Looking back at Johnny was a perfect reflection of himself. It was uncanny, the precise detail Willie put into the gray and white drawing. It wasn't Willie's immense talent, however, that captured the stunned attention of everyone looking at the portrait. In the distance, over Johnny's right shoulder, was the barely visible image of a small boy's face. His chubby cheeks were dappled with freckles, his infectious smile revealing a missing front tooth. He looked to be about Mickey's age.

"Benny," Johnny said softly as he reached out and gently touched the drawing.

"Who's Benny?" Boudreaux asked, afraid he already knew the answer.

"Benny. My little brother. That's what he looked like almost twenty years ago."

Johnny stared at Willie. "How could you know about him?"

"I don't know, Johnny." Willie said. "I told you. I just see things. I'm sorry if I brought up any sad memories."

"It's all right."

"What happened to your brother, Johnny?" Willie asked. "I'd like to know."

"I made it back from the war. He didn't. End of story."

"I'm sorry, Johnny," Willie said.

Johnny slowly stood, so Boudreaux could take his seat. "You're next, Boudreaux," he said, as he took a long drink from his beer.

"Okay," Boudreaux said, as he sat down. *Do I really want to do this? What dark secrets better left alone will Willie dredge up?*

"Ready, Boudreaux?" Willie asked as he placed Johnny's portrait aside and laid the blank sheet of paper on the easel.

"Yeah. If Johnny can handle it, so can I."

Willie stood in front of Boudreaux, studying his subject for several minutes. "I'm sorry, Boudreaux," Willie said suddenly, picking up the easel. "I don't feel up to doing any more drawings today. Maybe next time. I'm not feeling well."

As Willie abruptly turned to leave with his drawing equipment, Boudreaux brusquely grabbed his arm and spun him around.

"Baloney!" he said. "You were feeling fine a minute ago. What's changed?"

"Nothing's changed, Boudreaux. I'm just not feeling well."

"What do you see, Willie?"

"Boudreaux, I—"

"What do you see?" Boudreaux said, raising his voice.

"I don't think you want to know what I see," Willie said, pulling his arm away.

The others looked on in astonishment, not knowing what to do.

Jane put a hand on Boudreaux's arm. "Boudreaux, some other time, okay?"

"No. I want to know what he sees." He turned to Willie. "Please, you see something there. I need to know what it is."

With a sigh of resignation, Willie slowly set up the easel in front of Boudreaux. "Okay, Boudreaux. Let's get started."

Ten minutes later, Willie laid down his pencil. He slowly turned the easel around. Boudreaux was impressed with the likeness. *He really is good.* The drawing captured Boudreaux's handsome features.

Instead of smiling, though, there was a sadness in his expression. There was hurt in his eyes. That wasn't all. In the portrait, Boudreaux was shirtless, his shoulders covered with numerous scars, obviously from repeated beatings. The most disturbing sight was the presence of vertical bars partially obscuring his face. They were prison bars.

"I don't get it," Boudreaux said to Willie, who shifted uncomfortably from one foot to another.

Finally, Willie stood still and leaned in close to Boudreaux. "You may think you've escaped from your prison, but you really haven't escaped at all. You've just replaced your cell bars with others just as confining. I don't know what happened to you, Boudreaux, but whatever it is, you need to come to terms with it. I have a feeling hatred is keeping you locked up. As a war veteran, I've seen this in others. You can escape, but you'll need to find your own way. Until you do, I don't think you'll ever be really happy." He shook his head. "I'm sorry to bring all this up, Boudreaux, but you insisted. When you've succeeded in breaking those bonds, come back, and I'll do another portrait of you."

Willie picked up the two portraits and took them to a back wall. He searched for some unused thumbtacks, and when he found some, he pinned the portraits to a blank space on the wall.

The mood at the bar was somber as Boudreaux and his friends were lost in their own deep thoughts. Mickey thought about how much fun he had at the beach showing Johnny a world that was new to him. The Ozarks of Missouri were a long way from any beach. Johnny thought about the brother he had lost. Boudreaux was still trying to figure out what Willie was trying to tell him. Jane kept a close eye on Boudreaux and Johnny. She worried that the portraits Willie had drawn of them might reopen wounds thought to have been long healed.

The silence was broken by the laughter of two women coming through the front door. After patting their wind-blown hair in place and checking their makeup in their compacts, they surveyed the room.

Their eyes lit up when they spotted Boudreaux sitting near the end of the bar. They sashayed over to the counter, and the taller of the two, a brunette, sat on the vacant stool next to Boudreaux. She accidentally bumped her hip against his. The shorter one, a blond, sat next to her. She leaned forward and looked over at Johnny, trying to make eye contact. He ignored her.

They each ordered a glass of rosé. Jane and Mickey looked at each other and snickered quietly.

"Excuse me, handsome," the brunette said to Boudreaux in a husky, sultry voice. "Would you pretty please pass me that ashtray?"

Wordlessly, Boudreaux gave each of them a quick once-over and smiled. "I'd be glad to, miss," he said as he slid the ashtray over.

"Thank you," she purred, batting her oversize eyelashes.

"You're welcome, sir," Boudreaux said, returning to his beer.

"What did you say?" she asked in a voice that had miraculously dropped an octave.

"I said you're welcome, *sir*," Boudreaux said, putting emphasis on the last word.

The woman stood to her full height and glared at Boudreaux. "I'll have you know I'm a woman, not a man."

"Yeah, and I'm Tinker Bell," Boudreaux said, not in the mood to play games. "Why don't you and your cute little friend drink and leave us alone? The dresses, wigs, and makeup are nice touches, but those bouncing Adam's apples are a dead giveaway. Go bother some other poor suckers, will you?"

"You chauvinist pig!" she (or he) yelled, then knocked Boudreaux off his stool, leaving him flat on his back.

"Holy crap," Johnny yelled, as he leapt off his stool and went flying at the brunette.

They both tumbled with a loud crash to the floor. Johnny hauled off and punched the transvestite with his good hand, sending the latter's wig flying across the room. The short blond, not to be left out, jumped off the stool and landed on Johnny's back, biting and scratching.

"Get out of the way, Mickey," Jane yelled, as she took off like a shot after the blond. She busted her beer bottle over his head, sending his wig sliding across the floor, where it nestled alongside the other wig. "You bimbos—or whatever in tarnation you are!" she yelled.

While Boudreaux and Johnny sat on the floor in a daze, Jane tore into the two transvestites. "How dare you come in here and attack my friends!"

Willie stepped in and pulled Jane off their backs. "Hold it, little lady. I think they've learned their lesson. The four of you should skedaddle. Those two princesses have some pretty tough friends you don't want to mess with. They fight dirty."

"That's a good idea," Boudreaux said, dusting himself off and rubbing the bruise under his left eye.

They said their goodbyes to Willie and headed out to their car. They drove directly to the ferry landing. After crossing the channel, they continued their four-hour trip back to Whispering Hollows.

Jane drove silently, while Boudreaux and Johnny nursed their sore bodies and bruised egos. Boudreaux thought about Sachi. Johnny stared out the window. The full moon lit up the cotton fields. He thought about how much they looked like the clouds floating above them. Occasionally, he could swear he saw his little brother's face in those clouds. Mickey sat in the back seat staring at his mom. He was wired to the hilt from all the commotion. He would never again doubt the strength of that small woman sitting in the front seat. She was his hero. She had single-handedly—literally—rescued his uncles from those wild...whatever the heck they were. God, how proud he was of his mom.

Chapter Twenty-Three

"Johnny, I don't think we're in Kansas anymore," Boudreaux said, in a slightly high-pitched voice. They both stared in amazement at the towering green dome before them.

"What are you talking about?" Johnny asked in confusion. "I'm no geography expert, Boudreaux, but I don't recall going anywhere near Kansas on the drive up here."

Boudreaux gave Johnny a questioning look. "Don't you remember the tornado scene in the movie where—wait. Don't tell me you never saw *The Wizard of Oz*. It was a big hit right before the war."

"We didn't have too many movie theaters out in the boondocks where I was stationed. Even if there were, I would have been too busy peeling potatoes, digging foxholes, or marching to see any movies."

"Never mind. It's just an expression. I was thinking about how different this clubhouse looks compared to the one back home. This place looks like it was transported straight out of *A Thousand and One Arabian Nights* and dropped smack dab on the outskirts of Chicago."

"You're right," Johnny said. "It's pretty impressive. I guess they don't have the U.S. Open at just any old run-of-the-mill golf course. I don't think Whispering Hollows will ever be asked to host it."

"It is beautiful," Boudreaux said, admiring the elaborate architecture. "I can't wait to see the course."

It was a cool, crisp morning on the sixth of June, the Monday before the championship. Boudreaux and Johnny had just arrived the night before in Medinah, a small suburb northwest of Chicago. Medinah Country Club was the site of the forty-ninth U.S. Open Golf Championship, which would be held June 9–11 on Course #3.

Boudreaux and Johnny had spent the last fifteen minutes standing in the middle of the large semi-circular driveway. They gawked in awe at the imposing green dome above the entrance to the clubhouse and the two sets of smaller green-domed towers on either side. Behind them, bordered by the driveway, lay the largest and best-kept putting green either of them had ever seen.

"It's something else, isn't it, boys?" came a friendly voice from behind them.

They turned around, surprised to see a familiar face.

"Byron!" Boudreaux said, giving Byron Nelson a warm handshake. "You made it. You remember Johnny, don't you?"

"How could I forget? How are you boys? Suitably impressed, I imagine."

"More than impressed," Johnny said, shaking Byron's hand. "I've never seen anything like it. It looks more like the entrance to a palace than a clubhouse."

"This clubhouse, along with the golf course, was built by the Shriners in '23. It was designed to be a replica of the Shrine of Mohammad in Medina, Saudi Arabia. That's where it got its name. After the place was built, the surrounding community took the name of Medinah."

"I thought it looked like something out of the Middle East," Boudreaux said.

Byron nodded, looking around admiringly. "I've played here several times before, and I always look forward to coming back. Its architectural style is a combination of Italian, Oriental, Eastern, and Louis IV. I love it. Where are you boys staying?"

"We're staying at the Taj Mahal a couple of miles down the road," Johnny joked. "The desk clerk said that during the monsoon season, we even get running water."

Byron couldn't help laughing at Johnny's offbeat sense of humor. "I missed you boys. Most golfers I come across are stick-in-the-muds who take themselves much too seriously. You two seem to manage to enjoy yourselves every second. I'm glad you're here."

"Thanks," Boudreaux said, glancing at Johnny. "So are we. Byron, didn't you say you retired a few years back?"

"I'm semi-retired. I'm enjoying the life of a rancher, but I still like to come out for a tournament every now and then to shake the rust off. Of course, the U.S. Open isn't just any tournament. It's the national championship, and it's pretty special to me. As long as I feel I can compete, I'll be here."

"How's Ben doing?" Boudreaux asked.

"He's getting stronger every day. He wanted to be here in the worst way to defend his title, but he's still recuperating from the accident. With his will and determination, he'll be back someday."

"When you see him," Boudreaux said, "tell him we're pulling for him, and we appreciate all the advice he gave us."

"I will. He called me and told me to wish you boys the best. He said he'd get a kick out of seeing you take the whole thing with that funny-looking club of yours."

"That was kind of him to say that. I may just do it."

"I hate to run off, boys, but I still need to register."

"Me too," Boudreaux said. "We still need to walk the course and get a feel for the layout."

"I think you'll like what you see," Byron said. "Let's get together after the players' meeting tonight, Boudreaux. I'll introduce you to some of the other players."

"Thanks, Byron," Boudreaux said. "I look forward to it."

After Boudreaux registered, he and Johnny walked to the parking lot next to the clubhouse, climbed into the dust-covered Studebaker, and drove back to their motel. They decided to rest up before exploring the golf course. The motel was a far cry from the Taj Mahal. In fact, the run-down cottage they were assigned was barely a notch above the prisoners' barracks they occupied at Camp Fukuoka #17. They didn't mind though—they were in the U.S. Open, the most prestigious tournament in the country.

By midafternoon, Boudreaux and Johnny had walked the entire golf course looking for potential hazards. The perfectly manicured fairways, lined by towering red and Spanish oaks, bald cypress, and red maples, meandered through rolling terrain that offered breathtaking views.

As much as Boudreaux and Johnny loved the beauty of the Texas Hill Country, nothing they had ever seen compared to this. Boudreaux looked at Johnny to gauge his impression.

"Yeah, yeah, I know," Johnny said with a laugh. "This ain't Kansas, either."

Satisfied with their observations, they stopped for lunch at the clubhouse grill.

"I guess you have to be pretty well-heeled to belong to a place like this," Johnny said, looking around at the other diners in the room. "Look at the fancy duds these folks are wearing."

"I'm sure they put their gold thread-lined, satin undies on one leg at a time like we peasants do," Boudreaux said, in a passable imitation of a British accent.

"Cheerio, pip pip, and all that jolly rot, my good man!" Johnny scoffed, raising his pinkie, as he took a swig out of his beer bottle.

After laughing at the absurdity of two country boys trying to fit in with the likes of these sophisticates, they paid their outrageously high bill and went outside for a walk around the grounds of the club. They marveled at the sparkling swimming pool and immaculate tennis courts. They ducked back inside and explored the rest of the clubhouse.

They were amazed at the opulence of the high-ceilinged ballrooms and dining rooms. The elegant and imposing statues in the hallways made them feel as if they were walking through a museum.

That evening, Boudreaux attended the players' meeting in the grand ballroom. The tournament director explained the rules to the entrants and announced the groupings for Thursday's and Friday's rounds. Boudreaux looked around for Funaki and spotted him standing alone, looking out a window. Boudreaux was tempted to go over and tell him his little masquerade was about to come to an end, but resisted the temptation. He didn't want to cause a scene in front of so many witnesses. The time would come. Soon.

He saw Byron across the room and approached him. Boudreaux was astonished at the sight of so many professional golfers he had heard of and read about but had never seen in person. He wondered who he would get the chance to play with. There was the distinguished-looking Lloyd Mangrum, sporting his trademark mustache, who had won the Open three years ago. He overheard the tall, lanky Ralph Guldahl, who won the Open twice before, telling another player that this would likely be his last Open.

The short and stocky, yet powerful, Gene Sarazen, who had twice won the Open many years ago, was holding court among several younger players. Boudreaux eavesdropped as George Fazio discussed with Bobby Cruickshank his fervent desire to someday design courses instead of just play them.

Boudreaux was in golfers' heaven. He stood for a moment, mesmerized, soaking in the atmosphere of a little bit of golf history. *I wish Johnny could see this. He would be impressed.* Unfortunately, caddies were excluded from the players' meeting. Boudreaux would make sure to fill Johnny in on every detail of what he experienced here tonight.

As luck would have it, Boudreaux was put in a threesome with Byron Nelson and Sam Snead, one of the top golfers in the world.

"Sometimes, the tour officials like to place top amateurs with past major winners," Byron said, noting Boudreaux's excitement upon hearing the news. "The public really enjoys that. I'm sure you're aware of Slammin' Sammy Snead. He just won this year's Masters down in Augusta."

"Everybody's heard of Sam Snead," Boudreaux said.

"You and Johnny will like him. He spent some time in the Navy during the war. His jokes are a little on the blue side, but he's a colorful character."

"I can't wait to meet him," Boudreaux said. "He's always been one of my idols."

"There he is over by the window," Byron said. "Looks like he's got Horton Smith cornered, no doubt regaling him with the latest dirty joke. Come on, I'll introduce you."

Byron led Boudreaux over to where Sam was leaning against the wall, delivering his punch line. After the laughter died down, Byron touched Sam on the shoulder.

"Sammy, I'd like you to meet a friend of mine. This is Boudreaux James from Kerrville, Texas. He's one of the amateurs who qualified in Corpus Christi. Boudreaux, meet my nemesis, but good friend, Sam Snead."

"Pleasure to meet you, Mr. Snead," Boudreaux said, as he shook Sam's hand.

"Pleasure's all mine, Boudreaux. Please call me Sam. I hear the three of us are playing together Thursday and Friday."

"Yes, sir. I'm looking forward to it."

"You know, there's been a lot of buzz around the clubhouse about the new kid with the wonder club."

"Well, I'm still wondering if I belong here, Sam. This is a little overwhelming."

"It's overwhelming for all of us, Boudreaux. The press likes to build the whole thing up like we're all a bunch of big heroes of the golf world, but we're not. We're just ordinary guys who can't hold down a real job, so we're out here making the golf circuit trying to keep one step ahead of the bill collectors."

Byron laughed at that candid observation.

"He's hit the nail on the head, Boudreaux," Byron said. "Once you let the notoriety go to your head, you're done for. It's just a game. Treat it as such, and you'll do just fine."

"I've got to run, Byron," Sam said. "I need to work on my putting. I'm sure I'll see you boys during Tuesday's and Wednesday's practice rounds."

The three said their goodbyes and went their separate ways. Boudreaux found Johnny sitting at a table on the patio, sipping a cold beer.

"I wish you could have been there, Johnny, seeing all those big-name golfers under one roof. It was really something."

"I'll see them out on the course."

"I saw Funaki in there." Boudreaux looked around. "Uh, you didn't happen to see his wife, did you?" he added, a little too casually.

Johnny gave him a sly grin. "I think I saw her sitting alone by the pool, drinking a glass of wine." Johnny was no fool. He knew Boudreaux was smitten. "If I were you, Boudreaux, I'd keep away from her for now and try to stay out of his way. He knows we're the guys from Whispering Hollows, and, even though I'm sure he doesn't recognize us from the old days, I wouldn't push our luck."

"You're probably right, Johnny. Is my club cleaned and oiled and ready for tomorrow's practice round?"

"Yeah, it's ready," Johnny said, signaling the waiter for another beer. "And speaking of your club, what did you do to it? It feels heavier. And what's with the black electrical tape wrapped around the shaft? I saw you take it into Augie's workshop the other night after we closed. I tried to get in to see what you were up to, but the door was locked."

"I was working on something."

"It must have been important, since you didn't hear me knocking. From all the racket you were making, it sounded like you were operating Augie's lathe. And what was that awful burning smell? I was afraid you were going to burn the place down."

Boudreaux had heard Johnny's loud knocking on the door, but ignored it, because he didn't want anyone to know what he was doing. At least, not yet.

"I was working on the club's shaft," Boudreaux said. "I noticed a hairline crack near the hosel and was trying to fix it. I added the tape to give the shaft a little extra strength."

Johnny felt there was more to it than that, but knew Boudreaux well enough not to press the issue. He was sure Boudreaux had a reasonable explanation for his actions. He just shrugged his shoulders. "It's your club, but it's not always wise to change horses midstream."

"Don't worry, Johnny. I know what I'm doing."

Yeah, right, thought Johnny, suspecting this had something to do with Funaki. *I hope he doesn't do something foolish to get us both in trouble.*

Boudreaux's practice rounds on Tuesday and Wednesday weren't anything to write home about, but they gave Boudreaux and Johnny a chance to learn the subtleties and nuances of this difficult course. The fairways and greens were in tiptop condition. Even the rough was in better shape than the fairways back home.

Boudreaux finished his round Wednesday afternoon confident he could hold his own with the big boys. He and Johnny were a little uncomfortable, at first, with the curious stares from the other golfers and their caddies. Boudreaux was sure most of them had never heard of the Urquhart adjustable club, but he was looking forward to knocking their socks off when they saw what he could do with it.

At precisely eight o'clock Thursday morning, Boudreaux stood shoulder to shoulder with Byron and Sam on the first tee. The air was clear and cool as they awaited their introductions. Boudreaux's heart almost jumped out of his chest when his name was called.

"First off the tee, from Kerrville, Texas, please welcome Boudreaux James."

After a rousing cheer and thunderous applause from the sizeable gallery, Boudreaux smashed a beautiful drive down the middle of the fairway. Byron and Sam followed suit with great shots of their own, and they were underway.

Boudreaux played the course skillfully and closed with a one-under-par 70. Byron shot a 74. Sam finished with a 73. Boudreaux was thrilled that he shot the low round in his group. Byron was very polite and, despite some errant shots, was always the gentleman. Sam, a crowd favorite, liked to entertain his followers with jokes and wisecracks. Boudreaux had the time of his life playing with those two men.

The next day, Boudreaux fired an even-par 71. Byron ballooned to a 77, missing the cut and knocking himself out of the championship. Sam made 73 again, ensuring his presence for the weekend. After the round, Byron said goodbye to Boudreaux and Sam and wished them well. He said he needed to go pack his bags and get back home to feed the chickens and the cows.

"Give my best to Louise," Boudreaux said.

"That goes for me, too," Johnny added.

"He's one of the finest gentlemen I've ever met," Boudreaux said, as they watched Byron walk back to the clubhouse.

The final two rounds were to be held the next day, round three in the morning and, after a short lunch break, round four in the afternoon. In the event of a tie, an eighteen-hole playoff would be held Sunday morning.

Round three was a twosome. Boudreaux found himself paired with Cary Middlecoff, a twenty-eight-year-old dentist from Tennessee, who was at even par. Boudreaux was one ahead at one under par. Both were near the top of the leader board.

Boudreaux was surprised to see Funaki, who had been introduced as Arata Oshiro, in the group ahead of him. He was at even par. Boudreaux had been wondering when he would have the opportunity to confront Funaki and expose his despicable past to the world. *Wouldn't it be ironic if we were paired together in the last round?* Boudreaux thought. *What a grand stage that would be on which to exact my revenge.*

Watching Funaki's impressive shots from a distance, Boudreaux knew the man was playing well and would score a low number. Keeping that in mind, Boudreaux made sure he took his time over every shot. He took deep breaths to keep his muscles relaxed.

Boudreaux played like a man on a mission. He was on a mission, one greater than just winning the Open. He occasionally heard the explosions of cheering after Funaki's approach shots and knew his enemy was leaving the field behind. Boudreaux just concentrated that much harder. The better Funaki played, the better Boudreaux played. Glimpses of the leader board showed that it was now a two-man race for the trophy. He and Funaki were blowing away the competition.

Boudreaux finished the round with an astounding 63 to Funaki's 64. Boudreaux was now leading the championship at nine under par and Funaki was a close second at seven under par. Cary Middlecoff was in third place at two under par and Sam Snead was in fourth place at four over par.

The adrenaline pulsed through Boudreaux's veins. *It will be Funaki and me tomorrow. This will be a round the world will never forget.*

"You've got something planned," Johnny said, giving Boudreaux a hard stare. He and Boudreaux were eating ham and cheese sandwiches at a table in the grill, waiting for their afternoon tee time. The other players were scattered around the grill or in the locker room having a bite to eat and relaxing before the final round.

"Maybe." Boudreaux had decided the less he said to Johnny about his plans, the better. If things didn't turn out well, he didn't want Johnny to get hurt. This was his vendetta. He wasn't quite as forgiving as Johnny was.

Boudreaux had seen Sachi following behind the ropes, staying close to her husband. At one point, he had passed close to her and she smiled at him. He smiled back, noticing a fresh bruise around her right eye. She had made a feeble attempt to conceal it behind dark sunglasses. Boudreaux was angered by what he saw. *She's got to get away from that monster.*

At three o'clock that afternoon, the starter announced Boudreaux, who had the honors. He teed up his ball and hit a perfect drive down the right side of the fairway, staying safely away from the reachable bunker on the left. After his introduction, Funaki teed up and, with a graceful swing, put his ball in the middle of the fairway ten yards past Boudreaux's ball. He picked up his tee and with a graceful bow gave Boudreaux a smug look.

Pompous jerk, Boudreaux thought, as he smiled cordially.

For the next fifteen holes, Boudreaux and Funaki played on a level neither one had ever achieved before. They both had something to prove. Funaki desperately wanted to prove Asian golfers were superior to American golfers. Boudreaux wanted to destroy Funaki, on and off the course. He also wanted to save Sachi from this madman.

From their casual conversations, Boudreaux learned that Funaki remembered him as the hotshot amateur from Whispering Hollows. Luckily, he didn't know Boudreaux had been his wife's golf instructor. Boudreaux was also relieved that his unusual name didn't ring a bell with Funaki. Funaki had, so far, only referred to Boudreaux as Mr. James. The only light-hearted moment occurred early in the round when Funaki joked about the dangers of standing in front of Boudreaux when he was hitting.

Standing on the sixteenth tee, Boudreaux looked at the leader board and saw he and Funaki were all square at fourteen under par, way ahead of the pack. Disaster struck for Boudreaux a few minutes later.

The tee box on the dogleg left par four was a mere twenty yards from Medinah Road. A car backfired during Boudreaux's backswing, causing him to experience a sudden flashback to his combat days. He flinched uncontrollably, resulting in a horrendous shank that sent his ball sailing forty-five degrees to the right, plopping right into the middle of a pond.

The gallery gasped in disbelief. When Boudreaux regained his composure, he glanced over and saw a look of triumph in Funaki's eyes. *Don't celebrate yet, you sorry wife beater. It ain't over yet.* Boudreaux took a two-shot penalty and teed up another ball. He wound up with a double bogey on the hole, leaving him two shots behind Funaki, who made an easy par.

The seventeenth was called the lake hole. It was a difficult 197-yard, par three over a lake fronting the green. Funaki used a mid iron and landed his ball on the left side of the green, fifteen feet from the flagstick. A birdie for Funaki would likely knock Boudreaux out of contention.

Still a little shook up from his double bogie, Boudreaux took a little too long addressing his ball. Big mistake. The result was a topped shot, sending the ball in a line drive toward the middle of the lake. The gallery, who was rooting for Boudreaux, let out a collective groan. Funaki's face took on a smug look again.

It's said that miracles do happen at the most unpredictable times to those who, for whatever reason, deserve them the most. Maybe God was a golf fan who sometimes rooted for the underdog. Or, maybe God realized something more important was at stake today. No one will ever know the answer to that. But someone, or something, seemed to be looking over Boudreaux's shoulder that day.

When the ball struck the pond, it didn't disappear beneath the surface. Instead, it bounced twice, much like a stone, thrown by a child, skipping across a stream. On the third bounce, the ball hit the front of the green. It rolled uphill and slowed, until it dropped gently into the hole, giving Boudreaux his first ever hole-in-one.

The gallery went crazy, while Funaki gave Boudreaux a weak handshake and congratulations. Visibly shaken, Funaki walked slowly to the green where he two putted for par. Boudreaux and Funaki were even again with one hole to go.

On the eighteenth tee, Boudreaux had the honors. The ace buoyed his spirits and confidence tremendously, and he felt the championship was his. He nailed his drive down the center of the fairway with what should have left him with a fairly simple long iron to the green; however, the golfing gods weren't done testing him. When his ball hit the fairway, it hit the small outcropping of a rock dead on. Instead of the expected extra fifty yards of roll, the ball ricocheted straight back a hundred yards. *Oh, great! Now there's no way I can reach the green in two,* Boudreaux thought. Funaki's drive left his ball a good hundred and fifty yards past Boudreaux's ball, giving him an easy shot to the green.

"There's no way I can reach the green in two, Johnny," Boudreaux said, despairingly.

"Nonsense!" Johnny replied. "You didn't come all this way to lose the trophy to Funaki. I've seen you hit that ball a country mile. Even if you don't reach the green in two, you can still get it up and in for a par. You don't know what he's going to do with his shot."

"You're right, Johnny. Stand back. I'm going to give this everything I've got. If you hear a loud cracking noise, call an ambulance. That will probably be my backbone snapping in half."

Boudreaux took his stance over the ball, said a silent prayer, and took a big, wide, arcing backswing. At the top of his swing, he paused briefly then shifted his weight slightly to the left and brought his arms down with all the strength he could muster.

With a tremendous *crack*, the ball exploded into the air like a bullet leaving the muzzle of a rifle. For a few seconds, Johnny thought Boudreaux had, indeed, broken his back. He was relieved when he saw Boudreaux standing upright and his ball sailing toward the green. At first, it looked like the ball was going to land a few yards short of the green, but another miracle occurred. Perhaps there was a patron saint of golf, and Boudreaux was in his favor. Or maybe Mother Nature just happened to be a fan of good golf. Mysteries abound, even on a golf course.

Instead of the ball landing short, a sudden gust of wind arose and seemed to cradle the ball and carry it an extra fifty yards. Just as quickly, the wind died down, depositing Boudreaux's ball in the middle of the green, where it rolled to a stop two feet from the cup. The gallery roared again, as a distraught look settled on Funaki's face. Shaking his head in disbelief, he walked to his ball then hit it on the green, fifteen feet from the pin.

By this time, many of the other golfers and caddies had wandered over to the eighteenth green and joined the spectators to watch this epic duel between these two amateur golfers. When Boudreaux and Funaki walked on the green, there was a burst of applause from the gallery. The applause was soon replaced by murmurings as they stared in dismay at Boudreaux's club.

Boudreaux and Johnny looked down and saw what caught their attention. The club head of Boudreaux's adjustable club was tilted at a sharp angle. The part of the shaft just above the hosel had snapped in half, leaving the club head dangling from the shaft, held in place by a small piece of electrical tape.

"Oh, no!" Boudreaux said. "I hit the ball so hard, I broke the shaft."

"How are you going to putt out?" Johnny asked. "Maybe you can borrow someone's putter."

"I don't think that's allowed, Johnny." Boudreaux marked his ball and waited for Funaki to putt. After Funaki two putted for his par, Boudreaux knew all he had to do was sink this putt for the win.

Boudreaux replaced his ball and turned to Johnny. "It started with this club, and it's going to end with this club." He held his broken club up and looked it over for a few seconds before grabbing the club head and yanking it free of the shaft. He tossed the detached club head to the ground a few feet away, reversed the shaft in his hands and, with a serene calm, stood over the ball.

"What is he doing?" one of the other golfers asked in amazement.

Boudreaux lined up the headless shaft and carefully tapped the leather grip against the ball. It rolled into the dead center of the cup amid a chorus of hoots and hollers and cheering from the spectators and golfers surrounding the green.

After retrieving his ball, Boudreaux stood silently examining his club as if seeing it for the first time. His mind drifted back to that quiet evening the previous week.

When he was sure Johnny was asleep, Boudreaux slipped out the cabin door, carrying his Urquhart adjustable club. He hurried to Augie's office and, with his key, let himself in. He went to the back and entered the workshop that was used to repair and clean the members' clubs. He locked the door behind him. He didn't want any interruptions.

He laid the club on a bench and carefully removed the grip and the club head. He pulled the heavy, wooden bench forward and retrieved the wooden stick he had hidden behind it years ago. He then shoved the bench back against the wall. He turned this stick, which had been used to inflict immeasurable pain, over and over in his hands. *It started with this, and it's going to end with this.*

He carefully positioned it on the electrical-powered lathe. After several careful measurements, he turned the lathe on and carried out the first part of his plan. He was interrupted by a loud knocking on the workshop door.

"Boudreaux, you in there?" Johnny asked in a muffled voice. "What are you up to?"

Boudreaux said nothing. He kept working. After a few minutes, he heard Johnny leave the office. When he was satisfied with its final shape, he removed the stick and laid it on the bench. He pulled a small wood-burning kit from one of the bench drawers and plugged the cord into the wall outlet.

While the brass tip was heating, he thought carefully about what he wanted to burn into the stick before him. *The simpler the better.* Plumes of smoke drifted upward from the scorched wood as the letters and numbers took shape.

"It looks like you beat me, Mr. James," a familiar voice said, snapping Boudreaux back to the present. He stared at the man before him. Four years ago, the sight of this man sparked terror in him. Now, all he felt was hate and a desire for vengeance.

"No, it wasn't me who beat you today, Akio Funaki."

"You are mistaken, Mr. James," Funaki said, with a look of suspicion in his eyes. "My name is Arata Oshiro."

"Like I said, Funaki, it wasn't me who beat you today."

Boudreaux held up the broken shaft in front of Funaki and slowly peeled off the electrical tape, revealing the letters and numbers he had burned into the wood. By now, there was a subdued hush around the green as the crowd listened to this curious dialogue.

Boudreaux watched as Funaki's eyes widened in fear and understanding as he read the inscription: CAMP FUKUO-KA # 17.

"It was the spirit of the men you murdered at this prisoner of war camp that beat you today." Boudreaux said, his voice quaking with emotion.

"Budo!" Funaki whispered in astonishment.

"That's right. It's me. Budo."

The two men stared silently at each other for several seconds.

"The war is over, Budo."

"Not for me," Boudreaux said, his voice quivering slightly. "It will never be over for me. And I doubt it will ever be over for Johnny, either. Take a look at what you did to him." Boudreaux glanced at Johnny, standing a few feet away.

Funaki looked at Johnny, a spark of recollection in his eyes. "You cannot prove anything. It's too late for that."

Boudreaux brought the jagged end of the shaft to within a few inches of Funaki's throat. "Maybe. But it's not too late for me to kill you."

The crowd around them had closed in. There were accusations and threats.

"He's one of them war criminals," someone said.

"Murderer," said another.

"My uncle died in one of those POW camps."

"I spent two years in one, myself."

Funaki looked around in terror at the hundreds of pairs of accusing eyes condemning him.

Johnny grabbed Boudreaux's arm. "Not this way, Boudreaux," he pleaded. "If you kill him, they'll lock you up. What good will that do? What will happen to us? We're a team, aren't we?"

Boudreaux thought this over as he looked back and forth between Johnny and Funaki. He knew Johnny, with his declining health, probably wouldn't make it without him.

As the throng of accusers closed in on him, Funaki realized his only chance was to run. He'd escaped once before. Perhaps he could do it again. In desperation, he grabbed the shaft out of Boudreaux's hands and turned in an attempt to make his getaway.

As he stepped back, his left foot landed awkwardly on the now-detached Urquhart adjustable club head. His ankle twisted, and he lost his balance. He pirouetted in what seemed like slow motion and fell forward onto the shaft, the splintered end plunging deep into his stomach. As Funaki kneeled on the bloody grass with the shaft grasped in both hands, it looked almost as if the great and powerful warrior, Akio Funaki had committed hari kari.

Live by the sword, die by the sword, Boudreaux thought. He watched as Funaki twitched several times and fell on his side. The scourge of Camp Fukuoka #17 was dead.

After a brief police investigation, Boudreaux was cleared of any wrongdoing. Funaki's death was ruled an unfortunate accident. The press had a field day with the surprising turn of events when the sordid past of Akio Funaki, a.k.a. Arata Oshiro, came to light.

The next day, as Boudreaux and Johnny were packing their bags for their triumphant return to Whispering Hollows, they heard a knock on their motel room door. Boudreaux was pleasantly surprised to see Sachi standing there. He thought he would never see her again.

"I came by to say goodbye," she said tearfully, giving Boudreaux a big hug. "I'm flying home to San Francisco tonight. My husband's body will also be on the plane."

"What will you do?" Boudreaux asked.

"I don't know what my future plans are yet, but first I have to make accommodations to have my husband's body transported to his family in Japan as soon as possible. They are devout Buddhists and will insist on a proper funeral and memorial, after which his ashes will be interred at the family grave site. As his widow, I will be expected to attend."

"I'm sorry about what happened, Sachi," Boudreaux said. "It was my fault."

"I'm not sorry, Boudreaux. I hated him. I could never divorce him, so it's best that it turned out this way."

"Will I see you again?"

"Would you like to see me again, Boudreaux?"

"You know I would. I've been in love with you ever since I met you."

"I know," she said with a smile. "I've fallen in love with you, too."

"When you're finished with this family business, will you come back? I want to marry you, Sachi."

"Do we have a future together, Boudreaux? Could you marry someone from a country that was once your enemy?

I heard you tell my husband yesterday that the war will never be over for you."

"Give me a chance, Sachi. You could help me change."

"I have an idea, Boudreaux. Come to Japan with me. I can afford to fly us both there. My husband was wealthy, so money is not an issue. It will give me a chance to show you the real Japan, not the one you saw. Of course, we must be careful my husband's family does not see you with me."

"Of course. I'll go anywhere you ask, Sachi."

"I'll mail you a plane ticket to San Francisco as soon as I get home."

Sachi said goodbye to Boudreaux and Johnny, then turned and walked to the waiting taxi.

After Boudreaux closed the door behind him, he noticed Johnny looking at him with a silly grin.

"Remember me, lover boy?"

"Sorry, Johnny. I forgot you were standing there."

"If you hook up with Sachi, you're not planning on giving up golf, are you?"

"Of course not. I'm still planning on joining the tour. And you're still my caddie. That's never going to change."

"Speaking of change, why don't we get out of here?" Johnny said. "I'm getting homesick."

"Me, too," Boudreaux said. He held up the gigantic U.S. Open trophy with his name freshly engraved on it and gave it a kiss. "Cary Middlecoff might have won the $2,000 prize for low professional, but I get to keep this beauty for a year."

Two days later, the weary travelers showed up at the entrance to the Whispering Hollows Country Club with the Open trophy hoisted above their heads. Augie, Jane,

Mickey, and most of the members greeted them in delirious celebration.

Boudreaux stood on the bottom step of the clubhouse and looked around at the quiet beauty of the surrounding Hill Country. He clicked his heels together three times, and, in a slightly high-pitched voice said, "There's no place like home, Johnny. There's no place like home."

Johnny shook his head with a smirk. "Wait, don't tell me. *The Wizard of Oz*, right?"

Boudreaux laughed, as he turned and went up the steps. "You need to get out more, Johnny."

Chapter Twenty-Four

Boudreaux was shocked at the scope of destruction. Entire city blocks in and around Tokyo had been destroyed by the firebombing unleashed by the American bombers in the waning days of the war. What amazed him even more was the resilience of the Japanese people and their determined efforts to rebuild. For the past four years, there had been a robust explosion of new home and building construction and street repair. It seemed the Japanese wanted to put the war behind them as quickly as possible.

Boudreaux and Sachi strolled southward down the narrow street leading away from the Hotel Continental in Fuchu, a small town twelve miles west of downtown Tokyo. Occasionally, a pedicab or charcoal-powered taxi passed them, giving Boudreaux a feeling of appreciation for the ingenuity of the Japanese. He was surprised and impressed. Sachi explained to him that a shortage of gasoline forced them to cope in unique ways. Boudreaux's perception of the Japanese culture was slowly changing.

After a brief victory celebration with Johnny and his friends at Whispering Hollows, Boudreaux had dropped the bombshell that he was returning to Japan with Sachi for a brief visit.

"I think you're out of your mind, Boudreaux," Johnny had said. "You really plan on marrying that woman? She was married to our worst enemy."

"She's nothing like him, Johnny. I'm in love with her. Bringing her back here isn't going to change our plans. She understands that."

"I still think you're making a mistake, Boudreaux. We both still have nightmares of our time there. I'm afraid you're going to open old wounds."

"You're wrong. Sachi is sure my going with her and visiting her country will help heal those wounds. I won't know if that's true until I get over there."

"Go ahead, then. Just remember, I told you so."

Johnny wasn't alone in his sentiments. Augie and Jane were worried he might snap from the shock of returning to the land of his imprisonment. Mickey was afraid his favorite uncle would forget about him and not come back. Boudreaux had made up his mind. He was in love with Sachi, and, if accompanying her to Japan would assure her coming back to the States, it was worth the risk.

Sachi probably wouldn't have even returned to Japan if it hadn't been for her husband's family. As devout Buddhists, they insisted he be buried with a proper Buddhist ceremony. As soon as his body was received by his family in Tokyo on Thursday, a wake was held. The next day, a hearse transported the body to a crematorium, after which the ashes were placed in an urn and given to the family.

The following Saturday, exactly seven days after his death, the family would have a mourning at a Buddhist service. On the forty-ninth day after death, another mourning would be held. Upon its conclusion, the urn containing the ashes would be interred in the family grave, and the mourning would officially be over.

Sachi would then be free to resume her life, hopefully with Boudreaux. Sachi wasn't happy about remaining in Japan that long, but having Boudreaux accompany her helped alleviate the anxiety of seeing the family of the man she feared and despised.

The day Boudreaux and Sachi walked the streets of Fuchu was Sunday, the day after the first memorial. Boudreaux had spent most of Thursday through Saturday holed up in the hotel. Sachi had encouraged him to explore the area around the hotel while she was busy with funeral plans, but he preferred to wait for her to show him around. He was still a little anxious about how he would react to the Japanese he was sure to encounter.

"I have to remain here until the second memorial is over, Boudreaux, out of respect for the family. But I promise I'll come back to you afterwards. If you still want me."

"Of course I still want you. I love you, Sachi. I want you to become my wife."

"What will your friends think? Especially Johnny?"

"I'm sure when they get to know you, they'll be crazy about you. No one blames you for what your husband did."

When they reached the Tama River, they stopped and sat on the bank under the large, fan-shaped leaves of a gingko tree.

"I didn't realize your country was so beautiful," Boudreaux said, as he looked across the broad expanse of the fast-flowing river.

"You should see the colorful blooming of the cherry blossoms in late spring." Sachi took Boudreaux's hand in hers. "Cherry blossom viewings are celebrated all over Japan. It's a sight you would never forget."

After a brief rest, they stood and headed north in the direction of the hotel. For the first time, Boudreaux saw indications of the Allied occupation that had been in effect since Japan's surrender four years ago. Several American jeeps containing pairs of MPs drove by, the occupants wearing white helmets and white gloves. They slowed and eyed Boudreaux and Sachi suspiciously. Fraternization between Americans and Japanese was frowned upon by the Allied Command.

"How are the Japanese citizens taking to the occupation?" Boudreaux asked.

"They were fearful at first, but were surprised to learn American soldiers weren't the cruel monsters they had been led to believe by their military leaders. The American soldiers treated us better than our own soldiers did."

Halfway to the hotel, Sachi suddenly stopped and turned toward Boudreaux. "I want to show you something."

She took his hand and led him off to the right, down a side street. Ten minutes later, they stopped at an intersection, then took another right, this time down an unpaved alley. A few minutes later, they stopped in front of an old, two-story, wooden building.

Standing in the dark shadows, cast by the setting sun, Sachi motioned for Boudreaux to be silent. For several minutes, she intently watched the front door entryway of the house across the alley. Boudreaux looked up and down the alley and noticed all the houses were nearly identical with little space between them.

"What are we doing here, Sachi?" a confused Boudreaux asked.

For a several minutes, Sachi remained silent. A trace of tears formed at the corners of her eyes. "You never asked about my family, Boudreaux. All I told you was they died during the war."

"Was this your home?"

"For several years it was, but I had no real family here."

Boudreaux wanted to ask her more questions, but decided it would be best to wait for her to tell him what she wanted him to know.

"After my parents died, I was sent to live with my uncle's family. He was barely able to feed his own family, so he sent me here. I was fourteen."

"What is this place?" Boudreaux asked, unsure if he wanted to know the answer.

Sachi remained silent. Boudreaux saw a sadness in her eyes he hadn't noticed before. Before he could repeat the question, Sachi roughly grabbed his arm and pulled him back, deeper into the shadows. They both watched silently as the door to the building slowly opened. An old woman wearing a tattered robe emerged, smoking a cigarette.

"Mother!" Sachi whispered.

"You told me your parents were dead," Boudreaux said.

"They are. She's the owner of this building. The one we all called Mother. She was a cruel woman, Boudreaux. She treated us like slaves."

"I don't understand, Sachi," Boudreaux said, becoming more confused by the minute. "What is this place?"

Sachi turned toward Boudreaux and looked deeply into his eyes. "During the war, I was a survivor. Like thousands of other girls, I had to do whatever it took to survive. You can certainly understand that, Boudreaux. You were a survivor, too, weren't you?"

Boudreaux was beginning to understand. "Yes, Sachi. I was a survivor. How did you get away?"

"I met my husband just after the war ended. He said he loved me and wanted to marry me. He said he was a wealthy industrialist and wanted to take me with him to America. I had no knowledge of his military past. He told me he was an accomplished golfer and wanted to become a professional golfer there."

"Did you love him?"

"No. He was older than I was. He was a cruel man, but I would have married the devil himself to get away from this awful place. After he married me, he insisted on my taking intensive English lessons. His English was impeccable, and he wanted us to blend in as soon as possible when we arrived in America."

Boudreaux wrapped his arms around Sachi in a tight embrace. "We can talk about this some other time."

They retraced their steps to the street that led to the hotel. Several minutes later, they encountered a man sitting cross-legged in a doorway. He was emaciated and dirty and appeared to be in his mid-twenties. Boudreaux was surprised to see he wore the uniform of a Japanese soldier. Instead of the clean, crisp uniforms his captors had worn, this man's uniform was in tatters and hung loosely on his thin body.

Boudreaux stopped. He found himself unable to take his eyes off this man who looked back at him with a vacant, hollow stare. In front of the man was a battered metal cup containing several hundred yen. He made no attempt to beg for money, other than to give a slight nudge to the cup.

"Is this common?" Boudreaux asked.

"When the war ended, Japanese soldiers did not get the heroes' welcome that American soldiers received. Since Japan surrendered, their soldiers were looked upon as a disgrace to their country. Most found it difficult to fit in and find jobs."

After a few moments, Boudreaux reached into his pocket and pulled out a large wad of yen. He really had no idea of its worth. He walked over to the man and placed the entire amount into his cup. He didn't know why he did this, since he had harbored nothing but hatred for the Japanese soldiers who had made his life so miserable.

The man gave Boudreaux a slight bow. "Arigato," he said in a hoarse voice.

"Ieie," Boudreaux responded, bowing in return.

The man, pleased at Boudreaux's courteous response, gave him another bow and flashed a toothless smile.

"Boudreaux, these men were as much victims of our military leaders as you and Johnny were."

"I had no idea."

When Boudreaux had stepped off the DC-4 at Haneda Air Force Base four days earlier, he had expected the same look of hatred from the Japanese that he had received from the locals when he was on work details outside Camp Fukuoka #17. Instead, on his walks on the streets around his hotel, he was greeted with polite bows and smiling faces.

Was this why Sachi insisted I come to Japan with her? Was this her way of saving me as foretold in my dream? She said that Japan was moving forward with the help of the Allies and was appreciative of the Americans' efforts.

"I'm catching the plane back to the States tomorrow, Sachi. Are you sure you don't want to come with me?"

"I told you, Boudreaux, I have to attend the last memorial service on the forty-ninth day after my husband's death. Afterward, I promise you I will return to you."

As they reached the steps of the hotel, Boudreaux stopped and put his arms around Sachi. "I want to believe you, Sachi, but I'm afraid you'll change your mind. I can't live without you." He kissed her gently on the forehead, then they both entered the hotel.

The next day, they stood on the tarmac a short distance from Boudreaux's plane.

"What are you plans, Boudreaux?" Sachi asked, trying to hide the tears streaming down her cheeks.

"I'll go back to Whispering Hollows. Johnny and I have a lot of work to do if we're to make the professional golf tour. But first, I'm going to make a brief visit to a small fishing village on the Texas Coast."

"Are you going to do some fishing?"

"No. I need to see a man about a portrait."

Sachi gave him a puzzled look, then wrapped him in a tight embrace.

"Goodbye, my silly American. I'll come back to you. I promise."

Epilogue

The old man slowly meandered between the tombstones with a confused look on his face. He was having trouble remembering where a particular headstone was. His walking was encumbered by severe arthritis in his knees, but he refused to miss his annual trek to pay respects to his friend buried here four years ago.

For years he had relied on his cane to help him get around. Today, he had some help. A little girl with straight black hair helped him navigate the rows and rows of headstones honoring the heroes buried here in Fort Sam Houston National Cemetery in San Antonio, Texas.

His eyesight was failing, and he relied on the girl to read the names on the headstones.

"Here it is, Grandpa," she said excitedly. "We almost missed it."

Boudreaux squeezed the girl's hand, as he squinted and read the letters engraved on the tombstone.

JOHN W. FRYE
SGT
US ARMY
WORLD WAR II
FEB 16, 1915
SEP 13, 2004
SO LONG
SEE YOU IN THE FAIRWAY

"Was he a friend of yours, Grandpa?"

"He was the best friend I ever had. He saved my life."

Boudreaux released the girl's hand and squatted on his heels. He traced his friend's name with his trembling, weathered fingertips.

The girl grew impatient watching her grandfather reminisce about the past.

"Grandpa, tell me a story,"

Boudreaux turned to the girl and gave her a warm smile.

"Okay. But, first, I need to sit down."

They sat on a concrete bench under a towering live oak. Boudreaux placed his cane across his lap and gingerly scratched a thumbnail across the smooth, worn, shaft. Even with his diminishing eyesight, he could still make out the letters and numbers he had burned into the wood a half-century ago: CAMP FUKUOKA #17.

He reached into his pocket and pulled out the broken tee he had been carrying in his pocket for years as a reminder of days past. He turned it over and over in his hand.

"You want to hear a story, little Sachi?" he asked, looking affectionately into the beautiful, azure eyes of the girl who was the spitting image of her grandmother.

"I've got a great one for you," he said, looking off into the distance. "Once upon a tee—"

"No, Grandpa," Sachi interrupted. "Stories are supposed to begin 'Once upon a time.'"

"You're right. I'm sorry. Let me start again. Once upon a time..."

About the Author

William Willis is the author of *Base Jumping: The Vaga-bond Life of a Military Brat*. He lives in San Antonio, Texas with his family.

Colophon

The typeface Adobe Caslon Pro was used for the text of this book. The original Caslon type was created by William Caslon (1692–1766) in London. This old-world-style serif typeface remains very popular for print use because of its clarity and versatility. The digital version from Adobe was designed by Carol Twombly in 1990.

Also used in this book was the font Arial Rounded MT, designed and published by Monotype Typography in 1982.

The golf tees icon was designed by Freepik.

Book design and layout using InDesign CC publishing software from Adobe.

www.ingramcontent.com/pod-product-compliance
Lightning Source LLC
Chambersburg PA
CBHW030329030726
47499CB00003B/698